Simple Cooking for Smart Men

Simple Cooking for Smart Men

karen anand

Popular Prakashan
www.popularprakashan.com

Popular Prakashan Pvt Ltd.
301, Mahalaxmi Chambers,
22, Bhulabhai Desai Road,
Mumbai - 400 026.

First Published 2005
First Reprinted July 2006
Second Reprint January 2007
Third Reprint August 2009

(3973)
ISBN 978-81-7991-225-6

Book Design:
Awchat & Olsen Design
www.awchatolsen.com

Cover Photograph:
Nilesh Kale

Printed in India by :
Aegean Offset,
New Delhi.

Published by Ramdas Bhatkal
for Popular Prakashan Pvt. Ltd.
301, Mahalaxmi Chambers,
22, Bhulabhai Desai Road,
Mumbai - 400 026.

dedication

For my father Patrick, my greatest critic, who always said that I couldn't consider myself a cook until I could make a decent dal. Well. He who didn't know his way to the kitchen for the better part of his life...miraculously started cooking in his sixties. If he could do it, any man can.

thanks

A great many people have inspired this book. In the end, when you are alone with masses of paper to sort through and what seems like a never ending set of pages to edit... you can count the few hardworking souls around you on your fingers.

My thanks as always to my Publisher, Harsha Bhatkal who says "yes" to everything. To Swapna, for her speed, efficiency and encouragement. To Salil whom I have known since he was knee high and who today is a great cook (he says) and by the by...the designer of this book. To Ravi Menon, Arpan and Smita at Star One for getting so excited and commissioning Cook Na Kaho for TV. To Anil Naidu, Shagun, Gyani and the crew of Cook Na Kaho who were a constant inspiration.

To Piya, who kept saying, "where's the book ?"

To my biggest critics, the men at home... Yadu, Pogo and Sasha for constantly telling me what men would and wouldn't cook.

And finally... to my girls in the office... Sheela and Thangam. I couldn't have done it without you.

CONTENTS

FOREWORD

Men can cook? Or, can men cook ? That is the question. Men make the best chefs, I hear you say . Yes, they cook really well when they are paid for it. Catch any chef coming to the rescue in a domestic kitchen. Not likely. Having said this, there are certain cultures in which it is quite permissible for men to shop, cook and hold forth on culinary matters. They specially like to wax eloquent on the subtlety of a sauce or the 'nose' of a wine or the technical aspect of bread making. The Bengalis and the French are the biggest culprits, but others are fast catching up: young media men, middle-aged ad men, out of work intellectuals and "writers". They are all climbing on to a bandwagon, the food one, to which women have been strapped for too many years. Let's be fair, some of them are actually interested in cooking. Performing in front of guests has become a very attractive pastime. Few are actually bothered (I refer mainly to some Indian men I have come across) about where the ingredients come from or shopping for them themselves. But let's not discourage them, this is a start.

So, I decided to take upon myself the challenge of creating recipes and putting together a sort of "how to" manual for young men interested in finding their way into the kitchen.

A number of cookery writers today derive great, sometimes perverse pleasure in mystifying poor, would be cooks. They wax eloquent about unusual ingredients as if we should all use the "kaffir lime leaf" as part of our everyday vocabulary. Their recipes are a mile long with lists of ingredients which you will need the better part of a week to track down. Of course, they have no substitutes. You have to use exactly what they say: otherwise the dish simply won't be the same.

Then we come to the fancy utensils and the cooking techniques, all of which sound more and more foreign. Result — the newcomer to the kitchen is put off for life.

Food for me is a passion I would love to share. This is not going to happen if I suggest that you use gadgets which need a degree in computers to figure out and which will set you back a month's salary. What smart guys need to know even before they start cooking, is their budget, how many people they are going to feed and the time it will take.

A few words on what I consider "good food". I seem to have acquired the reputation of being "a fancy cook", tripping in and out of fancy five star restaurants. This is not entirely true. Unfortunately food is attracting the worst kind of snobbery. To me, food is either good or it isn't, whether it is from Singapore or Sholapur. Food is also about memories and people and places. It's the whole package. Not just what you actually consume. If you ask me what my most memorable meals are to date, what would come to mind immediately is probably something like a plate of prawns in a shack in Goa or a kebab in Bade Mian after a late night party. Dinner in a Michelin star restaurant in France may not even rank in the first 10. Why people feel that food in fancy restaurants has the moral high ground over a really good, well made kebab is beyond me. If both are good to eat and of great quality and they please you, then that is to my mind, good food.

Why cook at all, you may ask. Nigel Slater, one of my favourite cookery writers, has the answer. " You don't have to cook. You can send out for a pizza, queue for a hamburger, nuke a ready-made meal in the microwave, or book a table in a restaurant. You can pour water on a pot noodle, stop off for a Chinese takeaway or simply live on toast. I know this because I have done it. If you cook you will only have to trudge around the shops, get your clothes and kitchen dirty, have pots and pans to wash, your hands will smell of onions or fish and then everyone will only eat it anyway. Hours of work for minutes of pleasure. So why bother?

As I said, you don't have to cook. You can get through life perfectly comfortably without so much as lifting a wooden spoon. Fine. Do that. What I want to say is that if you decide to go through life without cooking, then you are missing something very, very special. You are losing out on one of the greatest pleasures you can have with your clothes on. Cooking can be as passionate, creative, life-enhancing, uplifting, satisfying and downright exhilarating as anything else you can do with your life... And to add to that buzz, the satisfying tingle that goes down your spine when you watch someone eating something you have made for them, and you have one of the greatest joys known to man".

The chapters and sections in this book are divided according to mood, need and circumstance rather than the more conventional "..starter, main course and dessert..". I have responded to needs and desires of that particular occasion and taken into account that today, rules can be broken.

I tried and tested hundreds of recipes on the four men at home, not to mention the ones I bothered in the middle of meetings with questions like, "what would you cook if you were taking Malaika Arora on a date?". I came to certain conclusions. Men love kitchen gadgets which do half the work, like a good food processor. Fair enough. So do I. Most women don't. For some strange reason, women of a certain age, love to toil and slave with blunt knives and old vessels to prove how hard they have been working. In some cases, I agree. By the time you get the tomato slicer out, wash and clean it, you might as well have cut the thing with a knife. But today's "cool men" need their basic tools in working order. Cool men also love a nice looking kitchen, not one that looks straight out of a Victorian novel (what the English used to call a "scullery") or a Siberian labour camp. They love quick recipes, easy shopping and like to see a smart table with smart accessories. The thing is that everything has to be made "simple". So here it is.

Simple Cooking for Smart Men.

SMART MEN MUST HAVE...

IN THEIR CUPBOARD AND FRIDGE

In an ideal world we would all be able to shop daily, like women in French villages carrying beautiful wicker baskets full of fresh market produce. On occasion, even I traipse around my local Shivaji Market (doesn't have the same ring as the "Marche Saint Germain", but never mind) in search of some goodies for lunch. Unfortunately, life isn't so simple, especially if you live in cities and work long hours. We have to compromise. This is where a small stash of fridge and store cupboard staples helps. They can form the backbone of the meal. I don't like to compromise on fresh fish, salad, and fruit. Today, supermarkets stock an amazing variety of ready to eat products, veggies, good quality cereals and grains, frozen foodstuff and imported ingredients. Even your local 'baniya' probably has all you need to whip up a quick dinner. It is all very well for 'purists' to go on about buying cupboards full of "essentials", which you are only likely to use once and which then rot until next Diwali. This can be both expensive and time consuming. Here is a basic list of what every guy should have, leaving out the overly exotic, ambitious and unaffordable.

SOME OF KAREN ANAND'S PRODUCT RANGE (...but of course !)

Basic Indian spices (whole)
Brandy (for medicinal purposes !)
Bread
Butter
Cheese (Spread and natural Cheddar - Britannia preferably)
Chinese Garlic Pods
Chunky Orange Marmalade
Classic Mayonnaise
Coffee (fresh ground and instant)
Cream (In small tetra paks)
Dal
Dal Bukhara (Kitchens of India) and any of their Curry Pastes
Eggless Mayonnaise
Eggs
French Dressing
Garlic Mayonnaise
Ginger / Garlic paste
Green Giant Corn tins whole kernels
Italian Dressing
Italian Pasta Sauce
Italian Pizza sauce
Maida or Atta
Milk
Mixed herbs
My range of Whole fruit Conserves and Marmalades for "brekkie"...
Noodle Stir-Fry Sauce
Noodles
Oil (Sunflower or Olive)
Olive oil
Olives, Jalapeños in jars (Tifys is available everywhere)
Onions
Orange Juice
Packet of Italian Pasta
Potatoes
Rice
Rum
Salt (preferably sea salt)
Soya Sauce
Spicy Mexican Salsa
Stock Cubes
Sugar
Szechwan Sauce
Tea
Thousand Island - Salad Dressing
Tomato Juice
Tomatoes
Tuna Fish Tins (Lakshwadeep is the best)
Vinegar (preferably natural red, white or sugar cane)
Wholegrain Mustard
Wine (one bottle of white and one of red)

SMART MEN MUST HAVE....
IN THEIR KITCHEN

If you open any foreign cookery book, you will find reams written on, "the right pan for this and the correct knife for that". Like the store cupboard, you will end up with drawers full of unnecessary gadgets (how often would you really use an apple corer, a thing to remove olive stones or an oyster opener?). Buy what is really essential and then let necessity dictate your next purchase. After all, you are the one who is going to cook with it. And don't believe that the most expensive is necessarily the best. Yes, of course, you tend to get what you pay for, but if that ten rupee potato peeler feels right, why buy the one that costs a hundred because it is "imported" and looks flashy. I am guilty of all of the above and have firmly learnt my lesson. So has my bank balance.

If you are going to cook you will need a few pans and a couple of knives, plus odd bits and pieces such as a strainer, tongs, etc, but don't be persuaded that you need a whole load of fancy stuff. You don't. It will just gather dust. As far as utensils are concerned, they can consume a lot of space, so really choose one or two only to start. I have a whole load of them but only really use three or four on an every day basis in a house which regularly caters for 6-8 people at lunchtime.

GIZMOS

Most men I know love gadgets. My idea of hell is a drawer full of those miraculous, time-saving devices specially designed for carving turkey or grating Parmesan. I know people with kitchens full of gizmos, none of which they ever use. Think before you get carried away on the internet or mall shopping.

And yet there are small things that make your cooking more efficient, economical or enjoyable. A blender for juices, soups and healthy shakes and an electric grinder for spices and wet pastes, are indispensable. Oven to tableware is very handy especially if it is studio pottery which looks much more special than ordinary glass. Saves you a lot of washing up dirty pans in the sink too.

Plastic air tight "dabbas" of various sizes to store leftovers (remember Mummy…)
`Pet` plastic jars to store spices, rice pasta etc. Bowls from small to very large for mixing (although glass is breakable it is odour free, easy to clean and scratch proof)
Sieve (large) for vegetables and pasta and (small) for tea
Set of steel tablespoons and teaspoons
Food Processor (preferably Philips)
Mixer-grinder (preferably Philips)
2 non-stick frying pans with lids (different sizes)
Cork screw
1 saucepan with lid
Set of measuring spoon and measuring cups
Paper napkins
Garbage bags
Paper kitchen roll
Knife sharpener
Brush for basting
Kadhai (wok)
Oven gloves
Cling film
Cake tin
Rice Cooker
OTG (Oven - Toaster - Grill)
Tongs (at least two)
3 knives (small, medium, large)
Simple crockery set
Glass measuring jug
1 handi with handles
Small tadka pan or small frying pan
Kitchen whisk
Wine glasses
Water tumblers
Potato peeler
Pepper mill
Tea cloths
Grater

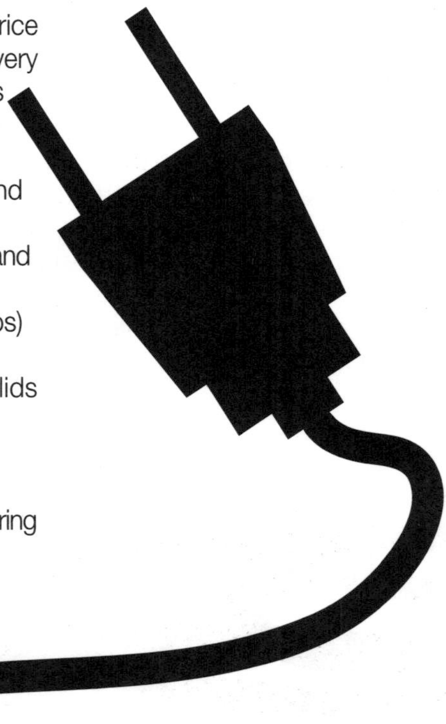

Food

FOR . . . STARTING OFF

1

FOREWORD

Smart men today are fit and aware of th looks. They are happier eating a balance diet of east and west than traditional, time consuming dishes.

The only problem is that, when it comes to life outside their mothers' homes or eateries, they have no clue. They love good food but have no idea how to cook, shop or manage a household. And cooking for yourself once you have decided to go beyond home delivery pizza and cuppa noodles, can be a daunting task!

So, in **Back to Basics**, I decided to give him simple recipes—the kind of food that he misses, a soup a salad, a pasta and a really flamboyant easy-peasy dessert which actually relies on a tin of Haldiram's Gulab Jamun.

In **Me and My Pans** I realized that guys don't have much in the way of utensils. So I have created international recipes which you can make in one frying pan — a complete one dish meal — a rice-based one, a noodle one and an all time favourite potato and egg meal-in-a-pan.

BACK TO BASICS

CLASSIC MUSHROOM SOUP / VEGETARIAN CAESAR SALAD / SPAGHETTI BOLOGNESE / GULAB JAMUN FLAMBÉ

CLASSIC MUSHROOM SOUP

Serves 4

INGREDIENTS

1 pkt button mushrooms (200 gms), roughly chopped
3 slices bread with the crusts chopped off.
1 clove garlic, crushed.
¼ cup butter.
2 ½ cups good chicken / veg stock.
salt and freshly ground pepper.
nutmeg or ground mace (pinch).
2 tbsps finely chopped fresh parsley
¼ cup cream.

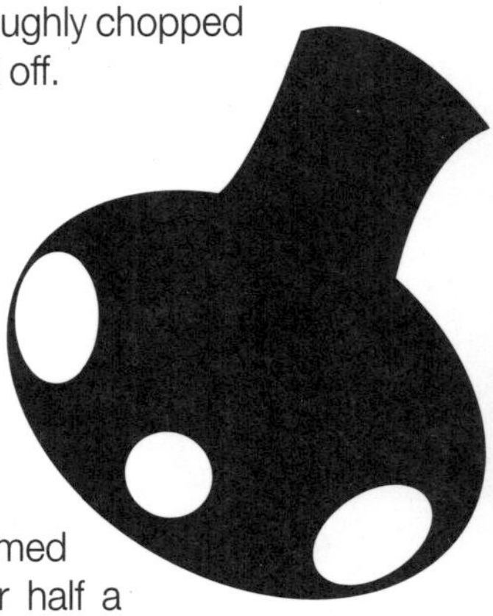

METHOD

Melt the butter in a large heavy-bottomed saucepan, add the garlic and stir for half a minute or so and then add the mushrooms. Turn them gently in the butter until they are slightly greasy. Put the lid on the pan and leave them to cook gently for 10 minutes or so. By that time they should be soft and mushy and the smell of cooked mushroom and garlic should be overpowering as you lift the lid.

Break the bread up roughly and add them to the mushrooms. Then add the stock and season with salt, pepper and a good pinch of nutmeg or ground mace. Bring the soup to simmering point while you stir it, and simmer slowly for 10 minutes. Liquidise the soup in a blender as rough or as smooth as you want. Return the soup to a clean saucepan, add the chopped parsley and cream and heat carefully without boiling.

KITCHEN ESSENTIALS

Sauce pan
Blender
Soup bowls

TIP

Never wash mushrooms. All you need to do is wipe them with a damp cloth. Always store in the refrigerator. When frying mushrooms, always fry on a very high heat otherwise they tend to lose their water and all you end up with is a soggy mess.

VEGETARIAN CAESAR SALAD
Serves 4

INGREDIENTS
2 heads crisp lettuce, like iceberg
6 asparagus spears, steamed
½ cup Parmesan or cheddar cheese, shaved (using a potato peeler)
3 tbsps watermelon seeds or almonds (slivered or sliced)
½ cup creamy French dressing
long slice of garlic bread made from a French baguette, cut vertically

FOR THE DRESSING
4 tbsps Karen Anand's eggless mayonnaise
2 cloves garlic, crushed
4 tbsps Karen Anand's French dressing

METHOD
Wash and dry the lettuce. Tear into bite-sized pieces. Refresh the asparagus in iced water and pat dry.

For the dressing
Put the eggless mayonnaise in a bowl.
Whisk in the French dressing and garlic. Place all the lettuce in a salad bowl. Throw in the asparagus, cheese, watermelon seeds and finally, the dressing. Toss at the table. Serve with hot garlic bread.

KITCHEN ESSENTIALS
Salad spinner
Glass bowls
Whisk
Large wooden salad bowl

TIP
This is a rather unconventional recipe for Caesar Salad based on the needs of pure vegetarians. The original one has anchovy paste in the dressing. To keep lettuce really fresh looking and clean, wash in plenty of cold water. Then spin in a salad spinner or shake in a big, loose tea cloth to remove all the water. Place in the fridge in a zip lock or airtight plastic bag. To make your own garlic bread, mix some butter with dried herbs, garlic paste and chilli flakes. Spread this mixture onto thick slices of French bread and grill until golden.

SPAGHETTI BOLOGNESE

Serves 4

INGREDIENTS

1 onion, peeled
1 carrot, peeled
1 celery stick (leaves removed)
3 big cloves garlic
½ pkt mushrooms
500 gms minced meat (mutton or beef)
100 gms bacon, rind removed, chopped fine (optional)
½ cup olive oil
2 tsps flour
1cup dry red wine
1cup chicken stock
2 jars of Karen Anand's pasta sauce
salt and pepper
freshly grated nutmeg

METHOD

Chop the onion, carrot, garlic and celery. Slice the mushrooms. This can all be done in a food processor in 20 seconds. Heat the oil in a large saucepan, add the onion, garlic, carrot, celery and mushrooms. Cook for about 3-4 minutes on a high heat or until the onion is softened, stirring all the time. Add the bacon if using. Stir for another minute. Add the minced meat and flour and stir for a minute or two until the flour is absorbed. Add the pasta sauce and cook until the meat changes colour, stirring. Add the wine, stock, salt, pepper and nutmeg. Bring to the boil. Lower the heat and simmer very gently for about an hour or until the meat is tender and the sauce is well reduced.
Taste and adjust the seasoning if necessary. Serve with spaghetti.

KITCHEN ESSENTIALS
Pasta boiler / handi
Sieve
Large saucepan
Plate to serve pasta

TIP
How to boil pasta: Bring at least 2 litres of water to the boil. Add one teaspoon salt and a drop of oil. Throw the contents of a packet of spaghetti or any Italian pasta into the boiling water and cook for approximately 12 minutes or until the pasta is firm to the bite–al dente. Drain and serve at once.

GULAB JAMUN FLAMBÉ

Serves 4

INGREDIENTS
8-10 readymade gulab jamuns with syrup
1 small bottle rum
1 tsp grated nutmeg

METHOD
Heat the gulab jamuns with their syrup over the gas. When the syrup starts to bubble, lower the flame. Meanwhile pour the rum into a metal ladle. Warm over a low gas flame.
When the rum ignites pour over the gulab jamun in a circular motion and set alight or 'flambé'. (Both gas flames should be off otherwise you will really be playing with fire!) Bring to table. Serve as is or with vanilla ice cream. Sprinkle the nutmeg. For some real 'pizzazz', throw in some fresh rose petals.

KITCHEN ESSENTIALS
Metal ladle
Gas to table dish

TIP
Gulab jamun must be kept warm either on low flame or in an oven in order to 'flambé'.

ME AND MY PANS

POTATO FRITTATA / SPICY SINGAPORE NOODLES / SEAFOOD PAELLA

POTATO FRITTATA

Serves 4

INGREDIENTS

2 potatoes
10 eggs
100 gms cheddar cheese, grated
2 tbsps finely chopped coriander
1 tbsp finely chopped garlic
1 small onion, chopped fine
1 green chilli, chopped fine
salt and pepper
3 tbsps oil

METHOD

Cook the potatoes whole in boiling, salted water until just tender. Cool, peel and cut into thin slices. Beat the eggs with the chilli, coriander, salt and pepper. In a non-stick frying pan, pour the oil and fry the onion and garlic until golden.

Pour in half the egg mixture. Arrange the potato slices on top. Sprinkle the cheese and pour the remaining egg mixture. Cook over low to medium heat until the mixture is set. Then place the frittata under a grill until golden brown. Cool slightly and cut into wedges like a pizza.

KITCHEN ESSENTIALS

OTG
Whisk
Handi
Non-stick frying pan
Mixing bowl
Serving plate

TIP

This recipe for Potato Frittata is also commonly known as Tortilla in Spain, which is a potato omlette often served in bars and cafes as 'tapas' or snack with drinks. The secret of a perfect frittata is to have it cooked through like a cake and yet not break it. In Spain, accomplished housewives fry it until crisp on one side, then place a plate on top, flip it over and slide it back in to the pan to cook the other side. It has taken me many years and many disasters to be able to get the timing just right. In the process, I found a much simpler way of achieving the same result without any mess and using a lot less oil. Fry the frittata in a non-stick pan with very little oil and then simply put it under a grill to cook the top. Make sure the handle of the pan is heat-proof first.

SPICY SINGAPORE NOODLES

(VEG)

Serves 4

INGREDIENTS

200 gms egg noodles (approx 1 large pkt), soaked in warm water for 10 mins, then drained completely.
1 onion, or 4 spring onions sliced
2 green chillies, sliced
100 gms bean sprouts
1 cup green peas, boiled
12 fresh spinach leaves, torn
1cup bean curd, diced and fried (you can substitute this with paneer)
2 eggs, beaten
¼ cup lime juice
2 tbsps Karen Anand's oriental stir-fry sauce
2 tbsps Karen Anand's Szechwan sauce
3 tbsps tomato ketchup
½ cup oil (sesame/olive)

METHOD

Heat half the oil in a large frying pan. Fry the onions and green chilli until fragrant. Add the peas, spinach and bean sprouts. Stir-fry until the spinach turns a bright green.
Add the oriental stir-fry sauce, Szechwan sauce, lime juice and ketchup. Stir. Add the noodles and bean curd. Reduce the heat.
Make a well in the center of the pan and pour in the remaining oil. Add the beaten egg and cook in the oil until set. Break up the egg and mix well into the noodles. Serve immediately.

KITCHEN ESSENTIALS

Large frying pan or kadhai
Big bowl to soak noodles
Bowl / platter to serve

TIP

The egg stage might be complicated for beginners. Instead make a thin omlette and cut into strips. Mix these strips with the noodles before serving. If you are not quick enough, your noodles may start sticking to the pan. Just sprinkle a little water to loosen them.

SEAFOOD PAELLA

SEAFOOD AND RICE COOKED TOGETHER

Serves 4

INGREDIENTS

2 cups thick grained rice (Kerala or Goa unpolished or "boiled" rice is perfect), cleaned and washed
500 gms seafood – large prawns, clams, squid, mussels
½ kg chicken with skin, cut into small pieces, or use boneless chicken
2 onions, chopped
4 tbsps garlic, chopped
1 jar of Karen Anand's pasta sauce
1 cup green peas (fresh or frozen)
2 red peppers, roasted and cut into strips
2 tbsps mixed herbs (parsley, marjoram, thyme)
2 tsps mild chilli paste (Kashmiri chillies ground with a little water)
1 litre strong chicken stock
2 tsps saffron, diluted in warm water
½ cup of olive oil

METHOD

Heat the olive oil and fry the chicken until golden. Add the garlic and onion and let it sizzle. Lower the heat, add the chilli paste and coat the chicken with this.

Throw in the rice, stir once and add the saffron and its water, pasta sauce and stock. Cook, covered, for approximately 25-30 minutes or until the rice is tender but still firm. Add the herbs, peas (if frozen, add directly) pepper strips and seafood. Check for seasoning. Cover and cook until the seafood is just cooked.

KITCHEN ESSENTIALS

Large frying pan
Serving platter

TIP

Seafood

Mussels and clams should be scrubbed clean and washed. When you add them to the Paella, they open automatically with the heat. If they do not open, discard before serving.

Squid should be cleaned and cut into rings. Prawns – if small, clean completely. Place some large unshelled ones on top for decoration.

For a vegetarian version – replace the seafood and chicken with cooked butter beans, artichokes and mushrooms.

For a quick version – boil the rice ahead of time in the stock with the saffron and refrigerate. When you are ready to eat, fry the chicken, onion and garlic. Add the cooked rice, chilli paste, peas, peppers and sauce. Heat through and add the seafood. Cover and simmer.

Food

FOR . . . THE PARTY SEASON

2

FOREWORD

Armed with your frying pans, my sauces and a couple of necessary gadgets, You are now set to take on the real acid test – your biggest critics – your best friends.

For **Guys Night In**, I created some finger foods which you can cook in front of them using ingredients available at the local supermarket. A little bit of `flash` here is Vietnamese meatballs with lemon grass for which you don't even need a binder like egg or bread.

Post "A-Big-Night" was a regular scene when I was a student. The proverbial "morning after", I should really call this "How to cope with a hangover" and "How to come up with a healthy breakfast in spite of feeling half-dead".

Then we have the biggest task – cooking for an actual party – at New Year. "Get them sloshed so that they won't taste anything", is one solution – or actually attempt some interesting snacks which will floor them.

Effortless Party Food showcases dishes which you can prepare in advance. Hummus can be made a few days earlier. The fish for the Thai Fish Cake can be steamed, made into patties and frozen only to be fried just before everyone arrives. The sauce for the Tomato Bruschetta can be made earlier too – Bruschetta is just a fancy Italian word for a crusty piece of bread. Bar the grilling of the chicken, for the Chicken Satay, the marination and the sauce can be done in advance. It's all a question of organizing yourself and your ingredients, so you're free to have a good time.

Guys love showing off their bar skills.
Cocktails is the perfect opportunity to do that.
Some are classics. Some easy, 'desi' versions would make any New York bartender sing your praises.

GUYS NIGHT IN

MASALA NACHOS / CREAMED MUSHROOMS ON TOAST / VIETNAMESE CHICKEN & LEMONGRASS MEATBALLS / SZECHWAN–STYLE PANEER

MASALA NACHOS

Serves 2-3

INGREDIENTS

3 papads, roasted or khakra
150 gms natural cheddar, grated
100 gms cream cheese
2 green chillies, chopped
1 tomato, chopped
1 capsicum, chopped fine

METHOD

Remove the cream cheese from the refrigerator and stand at room temperature for 5 minutes until soft and creamy. Break the papads into large pieces. Arrange on an oven-proof plate. Spoon over the cream cheese, chillies, chopped tomatoes and capsicum.
Sprinkle the grated cheese on top. Grill under a hot grill or in an oven for 1-2 minutes until the cheese melts and starts to sizzle. Serve at once.

KITCHEN ESSENTIALS

OTG
Oven-proof plate

TIP

Never use a microwave for this recipe as tempting as it may be. Your cheese will certainly melt but the papad or khakra will become soggy. Papad is a good substitute for tortilla chips which are not always available anywhere in the country.

CREAMED MUSHROOMS ON TOAST

Serves 3-4

INGREDIENTS

6 slices whole-wheat or white bread
1 pkt (200 gms) button mushrooms, cleaned and sliced
4 tbsps pepper cheese spread
1 tbsp butter
1 tbsp olive oil
½ cup cream
4 cloves garlic, crushed
1 green chilli
½ cup fresh parsley, chopped
salt and freshly ground black pepper

METHOD

Heat the butter and oil together in a frying pan. Add the garlic first and fry until golden, then add the mushrooms and fry on high heat turning several times until golden. If the mushrooms give off any water, continue to fry until it evaporates. Add the cream. Stir and lower the flame.

When the cream starts to bubble and thicken, turn the gas off. Add the cheese spread. Mix thoroughly. Season with salt, pepper, parsley and chilli. The mushrooms, cheese and cream should be a thick mass. Toast 4 slices of bread. Top with the mushroom mixture. Serve at once.

KITCHEN ESSENTIALS

Frying pan
Toaster / OTG
Plate to serve

TIP

Never wash mushrooms. All you need to do is wipe them with a damp cloth and store in the refrigerator.

Please remember to turn the gas off before you add the cheese spread or, if you forget, immediately afterwards, otherwise your creamed mushrooms will be "charred mushrooms".

VIETNAMESE CHICKEN AND LEMONGRASS MEATBALLS

Serves 4

INGREDIENTS

300 gms boneless chicken, with skin
1 tbsp tom yam paste
1 cup Thai basil leaves (optional)
2 lemon grass stalks (bottom white part only)
1 onion

METHOD

Chop the onion, Thai basil leaves and lemon grass stalks in a food processor. Put the chicken in along with the tom yam paste and mince the chicken. Refrigerate for at least one hour to firm up.
Form meatballs and cook in a preheated oven for about 10-12 minutes or until cooked. Serve immediately.

KITCHEN ESSENTIALS

OTG
Food processor
Serving platter

TIP

Choose chicken legs or thighs with fat and skin (never breast, since it is lean) because the fat helps to keep the meatballs moist, and acts as a binder. No egg or bread is needed to bind the meatballs.

SZECHWAN–STYLE PANEER

Serves 4

INGREDIENTS

500 gms paneer, cut into 1" cubes
½ jar Karen Anand's szechwan sauce
2 ½ cups thick coconut milk (tetrapak or made from fresh coconut, instant powder)
2 tbsps Thai fish sauce (optional) or salt
3-4 kaffir lime leaves, shredded fine (optional)

METHOD

Empty the Szechwan sauce and the coconut milk into a saucepan and heat gently for 5-10 minutes until it thickens. Mix well and add the fish sauce or salt to season.
Add the paneer and mix gently taking care not to break it. Sprinkle with kaffir lime leaves. Serve as is with toothpicks.

KITCHEN ESSENTIALS

Saucepan
Serving platter
Toothpicks

TIP

Kaffir lime leaves add a fabulous aroma to the dish. If not available, replace with lime rind. If you find the dish too spicy, add ¼ jar Szechwan Sauce or increase the coconut milk.

POST "A-BIG-NIGHT"

TAMARIND MARY / ORANGE SMOOTHIE / FLAPJACKS WITH HONEY OR MAPLE SYRUP / SCRAMBLED EGGS WITH CHEESE AND SPRING ONIONS

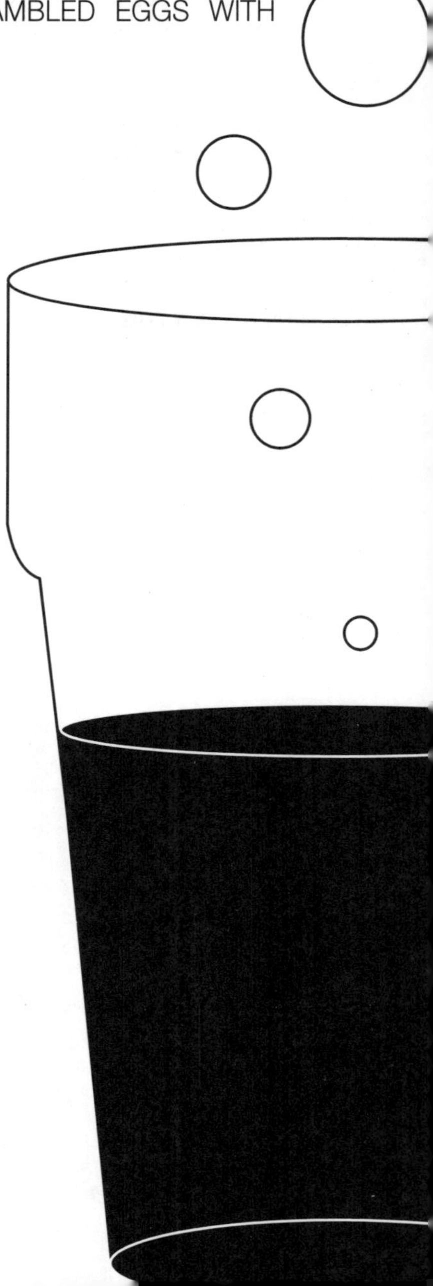

TAMARIND MARY
Serves 4

INGREDIENTS
1 litre tomato juice
½ cup tamarind pulp
¼ bottle flavoured vodka
lime wedges
roasted cumin dust

METHOD
Blend together all the ingredients, except the cumin dust in a blender or jug. Serve in a salt-rimmed cocktail glass. Sprinkle cumin dust.

KITCHEN ESSENTIALS
Blender or Jug
Squat glass / whisky tumbler

TIP
Tamarind juice
Made by cooking tamarind in an equal quantity of water. Add salt, crushed pepper and pinch of sugar and when thick, strain. Alternatively, use ready made tamarind pulp.

Flavoured vodka
Put 3-4 green chillies into a bottle of vodka and leave until flavoured.

Salt the rim of the glasses by rubbing the lime wedge along the edge and dipping the glass in a mound of salt

Cumin dust
Roast jeera until fragrant. Powder in an electric grinder, or with a mortar and pestle.

ORANGE SMOOTHIE

Serves 4

INGREDIENTS

400 gms yoghurt
200 ml skimmed milk
500 ml freshly squeezed orange juice
½ jar Karen Anand's chunky orange marmalade
1 tsp grated ginger
orange slices for decoration
plenty of ice

METHOD

Blend the yoghurt, milk, orange juice, marmalade and ginger in a blender, for 1 minute with plenty of ice. You may have to do this in two batches. Pour into glasses. Decorate with the orange slices, and serve immediately.

KITCHEN ESSENTIALS

Blender
4-6 Glasses

TIP

If oranges are not available, use tetra pak (preferably Real or Tropicana) orange juice.

FLAPJACKS WITH HONEY OR MAPLE SYRUP

Serves 4

INGREDIENTS

2 ½ cups flour
½ tsp baking powder
½ tsp baking soda
½ tsp salt
3 tbsps sugar
2 eggs, lightly beaten
2 cups milk
4 tbsps butter, melted

METHOD

Mix together the flour, baking powder, baking soda, salt and sugar in a bowl. Add the eggs, milk and 4 tbsps melted butter and whisk to combine. Rest the batter for 30 minutes.

Pour the batter with a ladle into a non-stick pan. When the flapjacks have bubbles on top and are slightly dry around the edges, (about a minute) flip over. Cook until golden on bottom, about 30 seconds. Stack the flapjacks and pour the maple syrup or honey over.

KITCHEN ESSENTIALS

Whisk
Mixing bowl
Non-stick frying pan
Plate to serve

TIP

Flapjacks can be made in advance and heated in a microwave.

SCRAMBLED EGGS WITH CHEESE AND SPRING ONIONS

Serves 3-4

INGREDIENTS

8 eggs (preferably `desi`)
2 tbsps butter
4 tbsps milk
2 tbsps spring onions, chopped
½ cup processed cheese, grated
salt and pepper

METHOD

Beat the eggs gently with the milk and a pinch of salt.
Melt butter in a non-stick saucepan on low heat. Add eggs. Stir with a wooden spoon until they are just setting (2-3 mins). Add spring onions and cheese. Season with salt and pepper if needed. Stir and serve immediately.

KITCHEN ESSENTIALS

Non-stick pan
Whisk
Mixing bowl
Plate to serve

TIP

The secret of perfectly soft scrambled eggs is not to overcook them. Remove from the gas when the scrambled eggs still look uncooked because they will cook further in their own heat.

EFFORTLESS PARTY FOOD

HUMMUS - CHICKPEA DIP / FALAFEL – BROAD BEAN RISSOLES / THAI FISH CAKES WITH SWEET CHILLI DIPPING SAUCE / TOMATO BRUSCHETTA / CHICKEN SATAY AND PEANUT SAUCE

HUMMUS - CHICKPEA DIP

Serves 4

INGREDIENTS

250 gms dried chickpeas
¼ cup olive oil
2 tbsps garlic paste
3 tbsps tahini
¼ cup lime juice
1 tsp salt
1 tsp paprika or mild red chilli powder to garnish

METHOD

Soak the chickpeas overnight in plenty of water. They should swell to almost double their size. Wash in several changes of water. Boil or pressure cook with a little salt in plenty of water until very soft. While still warm, put the chickpeas (you may have to do this in batches depending on the size of your blender or food processor) and two-three tablespoons of the cooking liquid, the garlic, tahini and lime juice into the mixer and grind. If the purée is looking too coarse, add some more cooking liquid.

Add half the olive oil towards the end. You should obtain a fine purée, which looks a bit like baby food. If you are going to use the hummus later, make the purée a little thinner, since it will dry out slightly in the fridge.

Serve in a shallow bowl. Scoop out a little from the centre with the back of a spoon or fork and pour in the remaining olive oil around. Sprinkle paprika or Kashmiri chilli powder on top.

KITCHEN ESSENTIALS

Pressure cooker
Food processor or blender
Bowl to soak
Shallow bowl to serve

TIP

The chickpeas have to be washed several times in water after soaking and before boiling. This avoids any excessive "gas" problems later! Hummus lasts in the fridge for upto two weeks.

Pita bread is a traditional accompaniment, if you can't find it, replace with Naan or Paratha bread, which you find in old bakeries.

In Lebanon, purists actually remove the outer skin of each chickpea by hand in order to obtain a really fine purée. I personally prefer hummus a little more coarse, so I leave the skins on.

FALAFEL – BROAD BEAN RISSOLES

Serves 4

INGREDIENTS

250 gms dried butter beans
2 onions, sliced roughly
½ cup fresh coriander
¼ cup dill
2 tbsps garlic, chopped
1 tbsp salt
½ cup sesame seeds
oil for frying

METHOD

Soak the beans in water for at least 6 hours. Wash in several changes of water and drain completely.

Grind all the ingredients together except the sesame seeds, in a food processor. Do not add any extra water. You will get a soft, green mixture. Shape into small round cutlets, roll in sesame seeds and deep fry in medium hot oil.

Serve with pitta bread, hummus and salad.

KITCHEN ESSENTIALS

Food processor or mixer
Bowl to soak
Frying pan
Plate for serving

TIP

Referigerating the mixture for a while and wetting / greasing your hands will make shaping the cutlets easier. If the oil in which you fry is too hot, your falafel will be black on the outside, your sesame burnt and the inside will still be raw. If it is not hot enough, it will absorb too much oil. One solution, if you are going to deep-fry a great deal, is invest in an electric deep fat fryer which keeps the oil at a constant temperature and actually reduces oil absorption into your products.

THAI FISH CAKES WITH SWEET CHILLI DIPPING SAUCE (TOD MAN PLA)

Serves 6-8

INGREDIENTS

1 kg boneless fish fillets (bekti, rawas or red snapper)
4 tbsps Thai red curry paste
100 gms green beans, finely chopped
1 tbsp, kaffir lime leaves (soaked 10 mins, then sliced, if dried)
2 tbsps finely chopped fresh coriander leaves and roots
1 egg, lightly beaten
1 tbsp Thai fish sauce
2 tbsps cornflour
1 onion, chopped fine
vegetable oil for frying

To serve

Fresh coriander sprigs
Sliced cucumber
Sliced tomato
Sweet Thai chilli sauce

METHOD

Steam fish in a sieve over boiling water. Cover with a lid. You may have to do this in batches. Test that the fish is cooked with a fork. Cool, then flake with a fork. Put fish and curry paste into a food processor and blend to a light, finely textured consistency.

Combine in a bowl with beans, lime leaves, Thai fish sauce, coriander, beaten egg, onion and cornflour. Knead with your hands until the mixture clings together well. (If it is a little too wet, place uncovered in the refrigerator for 30 minutes to chill and dry a little).

Roll into balls and then shape into 2" patties. Deep or shallow fry in a small frying pan or wok, a few at a time, turning them over if necessary to achieve an all-over golden brown colour.

Serve on a plate, garnished with coriander sprigs, sliced cucumber and tomato, and a bowl of Sweet Thai Chilli Sauce.

KITCHEN ESSENTIALS

Handi with sieve / steamer
Food processor
Frying pan or wok
Mixing bowl
Plate to serve

TIP

Can be made in advance and frozen. Steam your fish the night before. If it is still warm and soft, it may be too wet to make into cutlets.

TOMATO BRUSCHETTA

Serves 6-8

INGREDIENTS

¼ cup olive oil
1 kg ripe, red tomatoes
10 small cloves garlic, peeled and crushed
1 tsp sea salt
1 tbsp crushed chilli flakes
1 tsp dried oregano or a handful of fresh parsley or basil, torn
1 loaf French bread / baguette

METHOD

Plunge the tomatoes into hot water for 5 minutes. Remove the skins. Chop the tomatoes or run them through a food processor bowl and chop coarsely. Remove and put into a saucepan and cook for a few minutes until thick and pulpy. Heat the oil in a pan and add the garlic and crushed chilli. Fry until golden and add to the tomatoes. Season with salt and herbs. When the sauce is cool, store in the fridge.

Spread on slices of French bread as a starter or snack.

KITCHEN ESSENTIALS

Food processor
Saucepan or handi
Small frying pan

TIP

Pronounced, BROOSKETTA... a fancy Italian word for something on a piece of bread. This is a very simple tomato sauce. If you can't find really red tomatoes, don't bother with this dish.

CHICKEN SATAY AND PEANUT SAUCE

Serves 6

INGREDIENTS

1kg boneless chicken fillets cut into ½" thick 1" squares

Marinade

1 tbsp garlic paste
1 tsp turmeric
¼ cup tamarind pulp or lemon juice
1 tbsp oil
1 tsp cumin powder
1 tsp aniseed powder
1 tsp coriander powder
1 tbsp brown sugar

For Basting

Mix brown sugar, coconut milk and a little oil

METHOD

Combine all the marinade ingredients and coat the meat. Marinate for a minimum of 1 hour.
Soak bamboo skewers in water for an hour. Wipe dry and thread the meat pieces on to each skewer.
Grill in an oven or on a barbecue turning once. Baste occasionally to keep the chicken moist.

REAL SATAY SAUCE (FOR REAL PURISTS)

½ kg onions
150 gms garlic
2 lemon grass stalks (bottom part only)
1tbsp oil
100 ml tamarind juice
300 gms Sambal oelek or Karen Anand's Szechwan sauce
½ kg dry roasted peanuts, crushed
1 tsp garam masala
½ tsp cumin powder
½ tsp coriander powder
1½ cups coconut milk
1cup hot water
100 gms jaggery or sugar
salt to taste

Grind together the onions, garlic and lemon grass in a food processor or blender. Heat the oil and fry this paste until golden. Add the tamarind, spices and sambal oelek or Szechwan sauce. Stir well. Add the peanuts, coconut milk, sugar, salt and water. You may need to add more hot water as the sauce thickens very fast.

QUICK SATAY SAUCE

400 gms peanut butter
1 litre chicken stock
2 tsps garlic paste
2 tsps sugar
2 tsps Karen Anand's Szechwan sauce
100 ml sugar cane vinegar
1 cup crushed peanuts

METHOD

Mix all the ingredients together and cook on a slow fire until you get a smooth sauce. Cool and refrigerate.

KITCHEN ESSENTIALS

Bowl to marinate
Food processor
Bamboo skewers
Oven grill or barbecue
Saucepan
Serving plate

TIP

It is the peanut sauce, which is a bit time consuming, not the Satay itself. The sauce can also be used as a dip. Take care not to burn the sauce towards the end of cooking since it starts to stick.
Satays can also be cooked in a non-stick frying pan if you don't have an oven.

COCKTAILS

JELLO SHOTS / DIRTY MARTINI / PERU PYALA (GUAVA) / VIRGIN COLADA / CAIPIRINHA / CAIPIROSKA / FRESH KIWI MARGARITA

JELLO SHOTS

SERVES 4

INGREDIENTS

1 pkt flavoured jelly
1 cup / 200 ml water
1 cup / 200 ml gin

METHOD

Open a packet of any flavoured jelly into a bowl. Pour in 1 cup of boiling water. Stir to dissolve. Let cool to room temperature.
Add one cup of Vodka. Stir well. Pour into shot glasses (if you have them) or a bowl. Refrigerate until medium firm. Cut into individual servings and serve in shot glasses and knock them back.

Options: you can add finely diced fruits if you like and then freeze.

KITCHEN ESSENTIALS

Bowl
Shot glasses

TIP

Please try this recipe with at least two different brands of jelly before attempting to stun your guests. Different brands require different amounts of liquid to set. Use slightly less than is indicated on the packet. Basically replace half the liquid mentioned in the directions on the jelly packet with gin.

FILTHY MARTINI

Serves 2

INGREDIENTS

5 parts gin (Bombay Sapphire is the best)
1 part brine from a jar of stuffed olives
1 part brine from a jar of jalapenos
3 cubes of ice per glass
twist of lime rind
3 olives on a toothpick
1 whole (pickled) jalapeño, cut into 2, lengthwise, or a few slices.

METHOD

Place the gin in a cocktail shaker along with the two brines, ice and lemon rind. Shake away, or if you are a purist, just stir. Strain and pour into a chilled Martini glass and dunk in the olives and jalapeno.

KITCHEN ESSENTIALS

Cocktail shaker
Martini glasses, salt rimmed

TIP

The secret of a really good Martini is the ice. It should be crystal clear, rock hard and smooth so that the liquid can just glide over the cold blocks effortlessly. Use a small shot glass to measure one part.

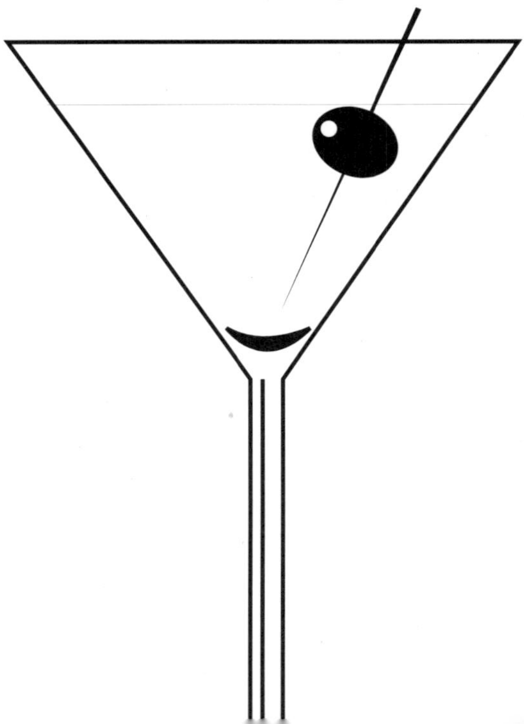

PERU PYALA (GUAVA)

Serves 2

INGREDIENTS

100 ml fresh guava juice or 'Real' guava juice
60 ml palm feni / vodka
4 drops Tabasco
a pinch of roasted cumin powder / cumin dust
lots of ice

METHOD

Blend together all the ingredients with lots of ice. Serve in a cocktail glass. Sprinkle with cumin powder.

KITCHEN ESSENTIALS

Blender
Cocktail glasses

TIP

Roasted cumin dust
Roast cumin until fragrant on a tawa. Powder in an electric grinder or with a mortar and pestle.

VIRGIN COLADA

Serves 2

INGREDIENTS

2 pineapple rings
1 cup pineapple juice
1tbsp lime juice
3 tbsps sugar syrup
¼ cup coconut milk
2 tbsps grated fresh coconut
Ice

METHOD

Pour all the ingredients into a blender, and blend until smooth. Served garnished with a wedge of pineapple.

KITCHEN ESSENTIALS
Blender
Tall glasses

TIP
If you manage to find tender coconut ice cream replace the coconut milk and sugar syrup with this. It will give you a creamier, richer flavour. For a Pina Colada, add 30 ml Bacardi and 30 ml Malibu to the above recipe and omit the sugar syrup.

CAIPIRINHA / CAIPIROSKA

(CACHACA BASED)
Serves 6 - 8

INGREDIENTS
20 limes
1 cup or more palm sugar or normal sugar
½ lit vodka / cachaça
lots of ice cubes

METHOD
Cut limes into 8 pieces and place them in a tureen. With the help of a muddler, crush the lime and palm sugar. Do this for some time and then add the vodka and the ice. Pour the whole concoction into old fashioned glasses (whiskey tumblers). Serve chilled.

KITCHEN ESSENTIALS
Muddler
Tall glasses

TIP
A mortar and pestle can be used to crush the limes. This quantity is ideal for a pitcher at parties.

FRESH KIWI MARGHARITA
Serves 1

INGREDIENTS
1 kiwi fruit, peeled and pulped
60 ml tequila
30 ml kiwi liqueur or cointreau
1 tbsp sugar syrup
3 tbsps lime juice
ice

METHOD
Blend together all the ingredients in a blender with plenty of cracked ice. Serve in a cocktail glass.

KITCHEN ESSENTIALS
Blender
Cocktail glass

TIP
If you add a little sugar syrup and lime juice to the kiwi pulp, you can store it in the fridge for up to a week.

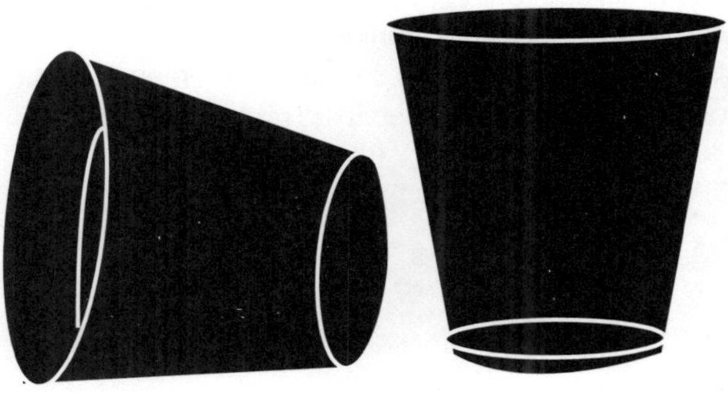

FOREWORD

When I asked a cross section of men about what they would choose to cook for a prospective girlfriend, **Date on a Plate**, they all came up with similar responses. Budget was no issue; neither was running all over town to find the right things to impress her. The pressing need is to "get it right" and guys are prepared to go to any lengths to achieve this. The only request was to "make it simple, fancy and quick" so that their short term goals could be achieved in the same evening, if possible.

Since we girls like to be wined and dined and pampered, I chose obviously expensive, special things like smoked salmon (caviar is stretching it a bit, especially if it turns out that she hates the stuff – which is quite likely). Roasting red peppers takes time which shows that you care. This can be done way in advance. Prawns in their shells are a wonderful finger-licking, sharing dish. And figs poached in red wine and tea doesn't just sound glamorous but can be kept for weeks afterwards just in case, you don't get around to dessert, or if she wants some more and is still around next week.

Wining and dining the Boss can be a tricky one, depending on the Boss. With one particular boss at Star TV in mind, I chose classic European dishes which require quality ingredients.

Putting it together like a Pro is fun – you have no time to cook – so you use the supermarket to provide you with ready made sauces and products. All you have to do is heat, assemble and serve. This is nothing to be ashamed of. Your guests have come to enjoy your company. They probably don't care whether you have personally ground the spices or not. If you can pull this off, consider yourself a "pro".

Christmas Special

Christmas is a great time of the year which lends itself to celebration. You have no choice but to attempt something quite lavish. Turkey is neither a tasty nor a glamorous bird and difficult to find in India. Use chicken instead, but don't compromise on the trimmings and the fanfare. Honey roast ham is a faff, but well worth the effort. Christmas pudding can turn into an easier task with the help of a food processor which chops everything up for you.

Food

FOR . . .SPECIAL OCCASIONS

3

DATE ON A PLATE

SMOKED SALMON WITH SPICY CREAM CHEESE / ROASTED PEPPER WITH GARLIC MAYONNAISE / GAMBAS PIL PIL / FIGS POACHED IN RED WINE AND TEA

Food or rather food and sex have been 'wicked' forever. Nothing new there. Food is passionate, exciting, seductive and sensual. We tend to 'woo' the opposite sex or attempt to, over dinner or a drink. Rarely does seduction happen over a chat about textiles or the share index. Intellectual pursuits just don't belong in the same basket as food or love.

Since 'sex' is a million dollar industry, we are constantly trying to find ways to make it better and to sell it more effectively. Food is used on more than one occasion on this agenda. Lobsters, oysters, bitter chocolate, ginger and chilli are the traditional things to get you going. Rare steak is supposed to do it for men. Salad for women. And you can always blame alcohol for all sorts of 'unbecoming' behavior. If you are either a teetotaler or a strict vegetarian, or both, you had better take to religion, science or yoga.

As we get older and more affluent, we also forget the simple and wicked pleasures of life. When you were younger, a bar of chocolate, a bottle of beer and the back of a car is all you probably needed to fuel the passion. As you get older, the mechanics of wooing become more complex, more subtle and more expensive.

I'm often asked by the press, usually just before Valentine's Day, to give apt recipes for the occasion. Consequently, my suggestions for a meal for swinging lovers, or for lovers about to embark on a career of swinging – will cost more than a bar of chocolate and a bottle of beer that used to satisfy and please us when we were simple girls. Today, we are mean 'chicks' who have high expectations. We want to be wined and dined in the finest restaurants, we want expensive gifts and an exotic holiday wouldn't hurt.

"I have no great faith in the advertised aphrodisiac qualities of certain food stuffs, because given the right atmosphere, you can become very passionate on sago pudding; just as you can remain frigid to a degree on a diet of peppercorns...But it is possible to achieve one's amorous ends by choosing the right food and the right drink and presenting it to the right person in the right way at the right time... There is one danger; when all is so carefully planned, Eros is inclined to strike before the fish course! This is a terrible waste of underdone beef, passion fruit ice cream, mint tea et al....For myself I think oysters are much overrated as a sexual stimulant. The last time I went to Wheelers and ordered half a dozen Whitstables only four of them worked". **Clement Freud**

So plan a simple menu for a simple meal which can be cooked ahead of time. Don't waste energy on trying to impress the other with your cooking skills, unless of course you are a galloping gourmet. As Ovid wrote, "Women can always be caught: that is the first rule of the game. If all goes well,... toast and ginger marmalade and some good hot strong coffee should be the next kitchen chore for you".

SMOKED SALMON WITH SPICY CREAM CHEESE

Serves 2-4

INGREDIENTS

250 gms smoked pre-sliced salmon
1tub (180 g) cream cheese
8-10 green olives and a little brine from the olives
8-10 capers
1 tbsp lime juice
½ tsp lime rind

METHOD

Keep cream cheese out of fridge for half an hour to soften. Put into a bowl with other ingredients except the smoked salmon. Mix well. Take a slice of salmon and put one heaped tablespoon of cream cheese mixture into the centre. Roll into cigars, tucking in the edges. Serve chilled on a bed of lettuce. Garnish with olives.

KITCHEN ESSENTIALS

Mixing bowl
Serving platter

TIP

The cream cheese filling can be made one day in advance.

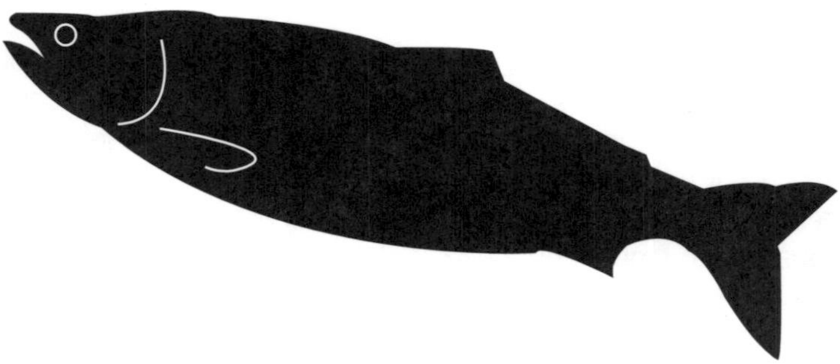

ROASTED PEPPERS WITH GARLIC MAYONNAISE

Serve s 2

INGREDIENTS

2 large red peppers
4 large cloves garlic, crushed
4 tbsps extra virgin olive oil
2 tbsps Karen Anand's garlic mayonnaise
salt and pepper to taste

METHOD

Wash and dry the peppers and score (mark with the point of the knife) the skin in a few places. Place in a preheated oven at 220°C. Turn occasionally until the skin begins to darken and split and the peppers look a little wilted. This will take 15-20 minutes. Cool and remove the skins. If you are lucky, the skin will come off in two or three pieces. Remove the core and seeds. Reserve any juice. Cut into one-inch strips lengthwise. Mix with the olive oil, garlic, salt, pepper and red pepper juice. For a really wicked salad, add two heaped tablespoons of garlic mayonnaise. Once roasted, peppers will last for up to a week in the fridge. Serve at room temperature as a salad or appetizer.

KITCHEN ESSENTIALS

OTG
Mixing bowl
Serving platter

TIP

Four to five peppers will take about 30 minutes. This can be done as much as 3-4 days in advance.
For a special flavor add two large green chillies along with the red peppers. Be careful when peeling them. Put them into a plastic bag to avoid direct contact with fingers.

GAMBAS PIL PIL

PRAWNS WITH GARLIC AND CHILLIES

Serves 2-3

INGREDIENTS

½ kg prawns, with shells
6 large cloves garlic, lightly crushed
4 Kashmiri chillies, roasted and broken
dash of white wine or lime juice
½ cup olive oil
sea salt

METHOD

Heat the olive oil in a heavy frying pan and toss in the garlic. Let the garlic sizzle. When it turns golden, add the prawns and fry on a high heat. Turn once. Add wine or lime juice, chillies and lastly salt.

If using large prawns, cover and cook for a further two minutes. Small to medium prawns need not be covered. They will take only three-four minutes to cook. Once they turn pink, remove immediately and serve hot with crusty white bread.

KITCHEN ESSENTIALS

Frying pan
Serving platter

TIP

When you use prawns with the shell and heads on, you must still de-vein them by cutting the shell along the back.

In Spain, this is often served as a first course with small shelled prawns cooked in an oven in individual terracotta dishes. If you don't like messing around with your fingers, buy small prawns with the shells removed, but the tails intact.

FIGS POACHED IN RED WINE AND TEA

Serves 4

INGREDIENTS

300 gms dried figs
¾ cup brandy
¾ cup dry red wine
½ cup honey
2 tbsps Karen Anand's chunky orange marmalade
1 cup of strong black tea, un-sweetened
juice and zest of two limes
½ tsp grated ginger
2 cloves
2 inch piece cinnamon
a few drops of vanilla essence

METHOD

Wash the figs in warm water, drain and place in a bowl.
Pour in the brandy, cover and leave overnight. Next morning, pour the brandy and figs into a saucepan. Add all the other ingredients and simmer for 30 minutes to an hour until the fruit is soft. The syrup should be like a thickish sauce.
Serve the figs cold or warm with a little syrup and some whipped yoghurt or cream on the side.

KITCHEN ESSENTIALS

Bowl to soak
Sauce pan
Serving bowls

TIP

If the figs dry out while cooking before they have softened sufficiently, add one glass of orange juice and continue cooking.
A great dessert to have at any time. Will last in the fridge for three months or more. In fact tastes better with time.

WINING & DINING THE BOSS

ROAST LAMB WITH ROSEMARY & ROASTED GARLIC / CHARGRILLED ASPARAGUS WITH CREAMY CHEESE / COQ AU VIN / POTATO DAUPHINOISE / CRÊPES SUZETTE

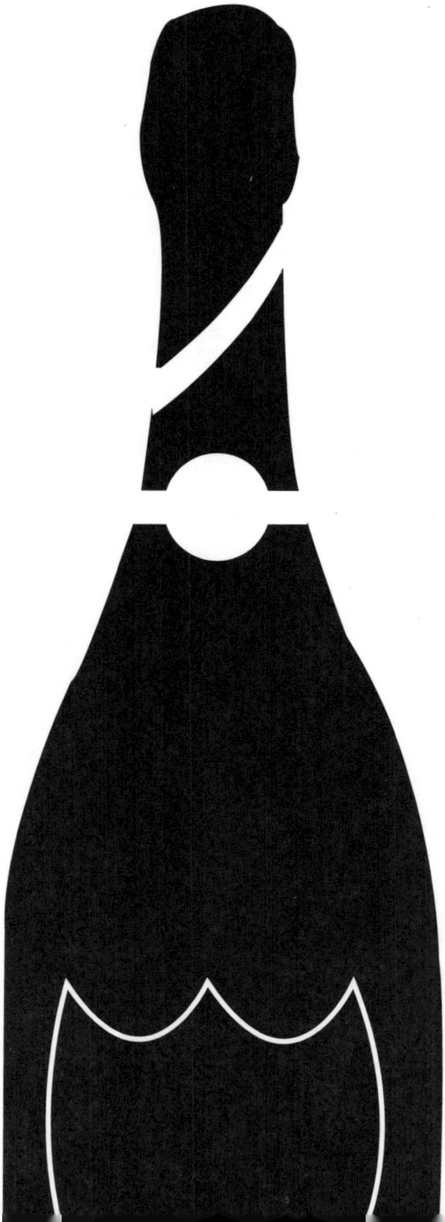

ROAST LAMB WITH ROSEMARY AND ROASTED GARLIC

Serves 4

INGREDIENTS

1.5 kg lamb on the bone – a leg preferably
6-8 sprigs of fresh rosemary or thyme
2 large heads garlic
1 head garlic, cloves separated
6 tbsps olive oil
½ glass red wine or 2 tbsps red wine vinegar
salt
crushed black pepper

METHOD

Put the lamb in a roasting tin big enough to allow you to get some herbs and garlic around the meat. Strip the thyme or rosemary leaves off their stems and chop or crush the leaves quite finely. Stir enough olive oil into them to make a spreadable slush, then crumble in some salt and crushed black pepper. Massage the seasoned oil and red wine all over the meat. Cut a third off the top of whole heads of garlic and place near the lamb. Pierce the meat with a thin sharp knife and insert the garlic cloves one at a time into the slits. Cover the dish and marinate for at least an hour or overnight in the fridge.

Set the oven at 250°C. Roast the lamb in the preheated oven for 20 minutes. Then turn the heat down to 200°C and continue roasting until the fat is golden and crisp and the meat is done, about 45 minutes. Remove the meat from the oven and leave the lamb to rest for 10 minutes before carving.

KITCHEN ESSENTIALS

OTG
Roasting pan
Mixing bowl
Serving platter

TIP

Lamb needs around 15 minutes per 500 gms of meat plus the initial 20 minutes to preheat the oven. This will give you medium rare meat, still juicy and quite pink in the middle. If you are using mutton or goat, pot-roast rather than cook in the oven. Use the same recipe, placing the meat in a large cooking pot with a couple of cups of stock or water. Cover with a tight lid. Cook until soft (about 1 hour at least). Brown in an oven for 10 minutes or so, just before serving.

POTATO DAUPHINOISE

POTATOES BAKED WITH CREAM

Serves 4

INGREDIENTS

4 large potatoes
1 tsp butter
1 clove garlic, crushed
½ tsp freshly grated nutmeg
200 ml cream
¼ cup milk
salt and pepper

METHOD

Lightly grease a shallow oven-proof dish with butter and sprinkle with the crushed garlic over. Peel and thinly slice the potatoes. Parboil them in boiling water for one minute. Drain well.

Arrange a layer of potato slices in the bottom of the dish. Season with salt, pepper and nutmeg. Whisk together the cream and milk and spread a little evenly over the potato layer. Continue layering the potatoes with the cream and seasoning, finishing with cream topping. Bake, uncovered (low) until the potatoes are tender.

KITCHEN ESSENTIALS

Oven
Oven proof dish
Mixing bowl
Whisk
Large handi
Serving plate

TIP

If you add the cream only on top of all the potatoes you will find that the layer at the bottom remains dry.

COQ AU VIN

CHICKEN IN RED WINE

Serves 4

INGREDIENTS

1 large chicken cut into 6-8 pieces, with the skin
2 tbsps olive oil
2 tbsps butter
1 packet (250 gms) bacon (remove rind and most of the fat) chopped
½ glass brandy
1 bottle dry red wine
½ cup chopped herbs (celery, parsley, bay leaf, thyme)
4 cloves garlic, crushed
1 packet (250 gms) fresh mushrooms, cleaned, whole
12 baby onions, whole, skinned
2 tbsps flour
salt and pepper to season

METHOD

Melt the oil and butter and fry the bacon and the onions. Add the chicken pieces. Brown on all sides. Coat with the flour. Set the brandy alight over a flame and pour over the chicken.

Add all the other ingredients to the pan, except the mushrooms. The wine should cover the chicken. Cover with a lid and cook for approximately 45 minutes to 1 hour. Remove the chicken pieces when done. Add the mushrooms and boil until the sauce thickens. Pour over the chicken pieces and serve with boiled potatoes or crusty bread.

KITCHEN ESSENTIALS

Saucepan with lid
Serving plate

TIP

Pronounced `COCK OH VAH`. Before the days of refrigeration, wine was used by the French to help preserve and marinate their meat. Soon after, French food became associated with wine sauces. It made interesting eating. Eventually, the cook of the house started to add other ingredients in the form of herbs, vegetables and aromatics and such prize dishes as Coq au Vin originated. If you would like to go easy on the wine, replace some of it in this recipe with chicken stock.

CRÊPES SUZETTE

PANCAKES WITH ORANGE BUTTER SAUCE

Serves 4

INGREDIENTS

12 pancakes
2 tbsps unsalted butter
½ cup castor sugar
juice of 2 oranges or 1 large tetrapak orange juice
juice of two limes
2-4 tbsps cointreau or brandy

PANCAKE BATTER

1 cup plain flour (maida)
pinch of salt
1 egg beaten
1½ cups milk
vegetable oil for frying

To make the pancakes, sieve the flour and salt into a bowl and make a well in the centre. Put the egg into the well and gradually beat in the milk to form a smooth batter. Beat in one teaspoon of vegetable oil. Leave to rest for 30 minutes. Make the pancakes. Pour a ladleful of batter into a hot lightly oiled non-stick pan. Swirl the pan so that the batter coats the bottom thinly. When the edges begin to curl turn out onto a plate. Stack them as they are made, interleaving them with sheets of greaseproof paper or non-stick baking paper. Continue until there are 12 pancakes altogether.

METHOD

Melt the butter in a large frying pan. Stir in the sugar and cook gently until it is a golden brown caramel. Add the strained orange and lime juices and stir until the caramel has dissolved and become a thick sauce. Drop a flat pancake into the pan, fold it in half and then in half again. Push to the side of the pan and add the next pancake. When all the pancakes are in the hot sauce, add the orange liqueur and set it alight when hot. Shake the pan gently to incorporate the flamed liqueur evenly in the sauce.
Transfer the pancakes to a hot serving dish, pour over the sauce from the pan and serve at once.

KITCHEN ESSENTIALS

Large frying pan
Mixing bowl
Whisk
Non-stick pan
Serving dish

CHARGRILLED ASPARAGUS WITH CREAMY CHEESE

Serves 4

INGREDIENTS

½ kg asparagus spears
½ tsp sea salt
½ container cheese spread
olive oil

METHOD

Brush the oven pan with olive oil and sprinkle salt. Place the asparagus on it and grill for two minutes on each side. Remove. Melt the cheese spread in a sauce pan with a little water, stir until smooth and pour over the hot asparagus. Serve immediately.

KITCHEN ESSENTIALS

OTG
Saucepan
Serving plate
Basting brush

TIP

Choose plump asparagus.

PUTTING IT TOGETHER LIKE A PRO

SEEKH KEBAB SURPRISE / BUTTER CHICKEN / DAL BUKHARA / ROASTED ONION RICE / APPLE & CINNAMON GÂTEAU

Cooking is about giving pleasure to ourselves and others. Some of us must, I suppose, get some perverse pleasure from standing over a stove littered with steaming saucepans, and being imprisoned by dirty dishes. I think that we are often guilty of turning dinner, particularly when we have guests, into a bit of a performance. It could all be so much easier.

SEEKH KEBAB SURPRISE

Serves 3-4

INGREDIENTS

1 packet frozen seekh kebab (approx. 6 pieces) [chicken or mutton]
oil for frying
1 packet Aashirwaad multi-purpose cooking paste
½ cup coriander, chopped
½ jar Karen Anand's pizza sauce

METHOD

Shallow fry or grill the seekh kebab and set aside. Mix the cooking paste with the pizza sauce and stir. Heat through. Pour the sauce over the kebabs. Garnish with chopped coriander.

KITCHEN ESSENTIALS

Frying pan
Serving platter

BUTTER CHICKEN

Serves 4

INGREDIENTS

400 grams boneless chicken, cut into 1 inch cubes
3 tbsps butter
1 packet of Butter Chicken curry paste (Kitchens of India)
3 tbsps cream

METHOD

Melt the butter in a pan and fry the chicken until golden. Add the Butter Chicken curry paste and one cup of water. Stir through. Cover and cook on a low flame until the chicken is tender (approx. 5-20 minutes, no more). Garnish with cream and serve with steamed rice or rotis.

KITCHEN ESSENTIALS

Handi / Saucepan
Serving dish

DAL BUKHARA
Serves 4

INGREDIENTS
1 packet of Dal Bukhara (Kitchens of India)
2 onions, sliced
2 tbsps fresh cream
oil to deep fry

METHOD
Heat oil and deep fry the onions till they turn golden brown. Drain. Keep aside. Heat the Dal Bukhara with one cup of water. Garnish with fried onions and fresh cream.

KITCHEN ESSENTIALS
Frying pan
Serving dish

TIP
Add one more cup of water or stock to the dal. It is often too thick for most people.

ROASTED ONION RICE
Serves 4

INGREDIENTS
2 cups Basmati rice
6 onions, roasted
1 inch stick cinnamon
3-4 cloves
2-3 black cardamom
1 tsp oil
5 cups water
salt to taste

METHOD
Place whole onions in a hot oven. Brush with a little oil and roast at a low to medium temperature until they are golden and soft (around 30-40 minutes) Remove. Cool, discard the skin which should be charred and chop the soft onion. Wash the rice and place in a rice cooker with the roasted onions, cinnamon, cloves, cardamom, water and salt. Cook until the rice is done (approx. 12 mins).

KITCHEN ESSENTIALS
OTG
Rice cooker
Rice platter

TIP
Roasted onions can be done in advance and kept in the fridge. If you really don't have the time or the foresight, use fried onions instead

APPLE AND CINNAMON GÂTEAU
Serves 4-6

INGREDIENTS
1 eight inch round plain sponge cake
6 tbsps Apple and Cinnamon conserve (Kitchens of India)
1 pkt Rich's whipped cream or 200 ml really thick double cream.
2 tbsps icing sugar

METHOD
Split the cake in half horizontally. Spread a generous layer of Apple and Cinnamon conserve on the botom half. Top with whipped cream. Press the second part of the cake on top.Take a fine sieve and sprinkle the icing sugar on top of the cake.

KITCHEN ESSENTIALS
Plate for serving

TIP
Conserves are basically high quality jams packed with whole or crushed fruit. These are better than ordinary jams because they contain a higher percentage of fresh fruit which lend a fuller flavour.

When you are in a rush, conserves come in very handy as fruit fillings for pancakes, tarts and puddings. You really can't get quicker than this recipe for a magnificent gâteau made in seconds.

CHRISTMAS SPECIAL

STUFFED TURKEY / QUICK STUFFED CHICKEN / HONEY ROAST HAM / CHRISTMAS PUDDING

It's the festive season again! This is when I throw caution, deadlines and all other work commitments to the wind and decide to have a good time myself (which usually involves large amounts of cooking) and share the festive spirit with friends. This year, I have dropped the idea of a formal sit down dinner with a huge turkey as a centre piece. There are a couple of reasons for this. Firstly, we are more in number this year, so the idea of a sit down, candle lit affair was just not feasible. Secondly, I don't have an oven big enough to fit a huge bird anymore!

Like the Americans, I will also be doing Honey Roast ham for Christmas lunch. These are not Virginia or Kentucky hams but the whiff of warm, smoked ham which has been cooked in a liquid of herbs, spices and beer, can be quite irresistible. The twist is my Orange and Mustard glaze made with our orange marmalade and wholegrain mustard. And of course, we have to have Christmas pudding, even in the afternoon, even if we're sweating away in the sun! We will also have a Christmas tree in the corner with lots of dangling shiny balls, pine cones and streamers and Christmas stockings for the children filled with lots of inexpensive little toys and sweets.

One thing I really miss about England is Christmas dinner. It's where British culinary skills really excel and for me it's more nostalgia than anything else. If you have ever lived in England, you will know that Christmas dinner is as full of idiosyncrasies as other British traits: the mystery surrounding the Chipolata Sausage and the Turkey; the Cubist theory behind the uneven potatoes; and where do the Brussels sprouts and the bread sauce fit in? And the only conclusion I came to was that tradition, in this case, is somewhat inexplicable. Let's just put it down to British eccentricity, which is at its best during Christmas. This is when all those little quirks can be let out of the closet shamelessly. The British are proud of Christmas and so they should be! This is about the only time of year when they are allowed to show off their great gastronomic delights for all to ogle at. And anyone who has suffered at the hands of British cooks will tell you that this is the one time of year when you'll find anything half way edible on a British table!

STUFFED TURKEY

Serves 8

INGREDIENTS

3 kg Turkey, well cleaned
3 tbsps extra virgin olive oil
10 fresh sage leaves, or 2 tsps dry sage
coarse sea salt
3 tbsps unsalted butter, melted for basting
1½ cups of dry white wine

CLASSIC STUFFING 1

Ingredients

6 tbsps butter
2 onions, diced
4 celery stalks, diced
5 fresh sage leaves, chopped or 1 tsp crushed dry sage
2 cups chicken stock
½ loaf old white bread
1 tsp freshly ground black pepper
1 cup coarsely, chopped parsley leaves
½ tsp salt

METHOD

For the stuffing

Melt the butter in a large frying pan. Add the onions and celery and cook over medium heat until the onions are translucent, about 8 minutes. Add the carrots and sausages. Add the sage, stir to combine and cook for 3 minutes.

Add half-cup stock and stir well. Cook for about 5 minutes until the liquid has reduced by half. Transfer the onion mixture to a large mixing bowl. Add the bread, salt, pepper, parsley and the remaining one and a half cups of stock. Mix to combine. Use to stuff the chicken immediately.

For the turkey

Preheat the oven to 180°C. Rinse the bird thoroughly with water. Pat dry. Rub the olive oil over the entire surface of the turkey. Using your fingers, gently loosen the skin of the turkey from breast and drum sticks. Carefully arrange individual layers of sage under the skin. Lightly salt the cavity. Turn the turkey breast side down and loosely stuff the neck cavity with about two cups of classic stuffing. Pull the neck skin over the cavity and fasten it to the back of the turkey with skewers or wooden picks.

Turn the turkey breast side up and fold the wing tips underneath the turkey so that the tips are almost touching. Lightly stuff the main cavity with stuffing. Place a double layer of aluminium foil over the exposed stuffing and tie the drum sticks together with kitchen string. Place the turkey on a rack in a large roasting pan lined with aluminium foil and generously brush with melted butter.

Roast the turkey basting every thirty minutes with melted butter and pan juices, for about 2½ hours. During the last half hour add the dry white wine to the pan. If the turkey legs or breast brown too quickly, cover them lightly with foil.

Transfer the turkey to a cutting board, reserving the pan juices for gravy. Remove the stuffing, tent the turkey with foil, and allow it to sit for 20–30 minutes before carving.

KITCHEN ESSENTIALS

Oven
Roasting tin
Frying Pan
Large mixing bowl

QUICK STUFFED CHICKEN

(A Christmas alternative when you don't have an oven big enough for a turkey.)

Serves 4

INGREDIENTS

1 chicken, weighing approx. 1.2 kg (completely clean inside, with no offal)
3 tbsps extra virgin olive oil
coarse sea salt
3 tbsps butter, melted for basting
1½ cups of dry white wine

CLASSIC STUFFING 2
Ingredients

6 tbsps butter
2 onions, diced
4 celery stalks, diced
1 tsp dried sage
2 carrots, diced
4 chicken sausages, diced
2 cups chicken stock
½ loaf old white bread
½ tsp salt
1 tsp freshly ground black pepper
1 cup coarsely chopped parsley leaves

METHOD

For the stuffing

Melt the butter in a large frying pan. Add the onions and celery and cook over medium heat until the onions are translucent, about 8 minutes. Add the carrots and sausages. Add the sage, stir to combine and cook for 3 minutes.

Add half-cup stock and stir well. Cook for about 5 minutes until the liquid has reduced by half. Transfer the onion mixture to a large mixing bowl. Add the bread, salt, pepper, parsley and the remaining one and a half cups of stock. Mix to combine. Use to stuff the chicken immediately.

For the stuffed chicken

Preheat the oven to 180°C. Rinse the bird thoroughly with water. Pat dry. Rub the olive oil over the entire surface of the chicken. Lightly salt the cavity. Turn the chicken breast side down and loosely stuff the neck cavity with classic stuffing.

Pull the neck skin over the cavity and fasten it to the back of the chicken with tooth picks.Turn the chicken breast side up and fold the wing tips underneath the chicken so that the tips are almost touching. Lightly stuff the main cavity with stuffing.

Place a double layer of aluminum foil over the exposed stuffing and tie the drum sticks together with kitchen string. Place the chicken on a rack in a large roasting pan lined with aluminium foil and generously brush with melted butter. Pour the white wine into the pan

Roast the chicken basting every ten minutes with melted butter and pan juices, for about 1 hour. Carve the chicken at the table.

HONEY ROAST HAM

Serves 6-8

INGREDIENTS

1 smoked ham (approx. 3 kgs with bone)
2 bottles of stout or strong beer
1 tsp black pepper corn
3 onions, sliced
1 stick cinnamon
1 tsp clove
2 bay leaves
1 cup sugar

GLAZE

2 tbsps Karen Anand's chunky orange marmalade
2 tbsps Karen Anand's whole grain mustard

METHOD

Put the ham in a large handi with all the ingredients. Add water to cover. Bring to the boil and simmer until the ham is soft. This will take approximately one and a half hours. Remove when cool enough to handle. Carefully pull off the skin taking care not to pull off the fat. You may need to use a small sharp knife to do this successfully.
Score the fat in diagonal criss cross lines. Mix all the ingredients for the glaze in a bowl and rub all over the ham generously. Preheat the oven to 180ºC and roast the ham for 20 minutes to half an hour or until the fat is golden and a little crispy. Remove, slice and serve.

KITCHEN ESSENTIALS

Large handi
OTG
Mixing bowl
Serving plate

TIP

This is a laborious recipe but well worth it for the excitement it will create. Cook the ham well in advance and freeze. Just before Christmas thaw the ham, take off skin and glaze. Then it doesn't seem like such an effort.

CHRISTMAS PUDDING

Serves 16 (makes 4 large puddings)

INGREDIENTS

100 gms (1cup) almonds
120 gms (1 cup) sultanas (yellow raisins)
120 gms (1 cup) currants (black raisins)
300 gms (2 cups) raisins (brown)
100 gms (3/4 cup) Karen Anand's chunky orange marmalde
250 gms fine fresh breadcrumbs
180 gms (1¼ cups) butter
2 tbsps cocoa
180 gms (2 cups) plain flour
3 tsps baking powder and a pinch of salt
2 tsps mixed spice (mace, cardamom, cloves, allspice), ground to a powder
2 tsps grated nutmeg,
1 tsp cinnamon, powdered
400 gms (2 cups) brown sugar
juice and rind of 2 limes
6 eggs
½ cup milk
½ bottle brandy
¼ bottle rum

METHOD

Wash all the dried fruit. Dry thoroughly. Remove seeds, if necessary, and chop in a food processor. Any other way is simply too time consuming and you are likely to lose interest in the recipe at this stage. Soak overnight with rum and half the brandy. Blanch and chop almonds (also in the processor). Grate butter from the fridge. Sieve the flour, coca and spices. Add brown sugar, juice and rind of limes, butter, almonds, breadcrumbs, marmalade and dried fruit. Stir well. Stir in the eggs, milk, and remaining brandy. Set aside for two hours.

Put the mixture into greased pudding moulds (preferably glass or ceramic). Leave one inch from the top to expand. Tie with greaseproof paper or foil and then a piece of muslin. Place all the puddings in a large vessel (handi). Pour in enough water to come two-thirds of the way up the puddings. Let the water come to a rolling boil and then reduce the heat slightly. Cover with a lid and steam for four-five hours. You may need to top up with water during cooking, since the bowls must always be two-thirds submerged in water. When cooked, remove from the water and store in a cool place (not a fridge).

The puddings should last at least three months. They can be re-heated by steaming once more or heated in a microwave on high for three minutes. Serve warm with cream.

KITCHEN ESSENTIALS

Food processor
Large bowl
Small bowls
Big handi to steam

TIP

Most Christmas pudding needs to be made months in advance.
I have neither the time nor the organizational skills to plan my life nor my kitchen that much in advance. This recipe can be made three days in advance and tastes amazingly good except that it comes out dark brown and not black.

When Christmas was a family affair in Britain, it was the kind of thing that memories are made of. A huge Christmas tree in the corner with lots of dangling shiny balls, pine cones and streamers, Christmas stockings filled with lots of inexpensive little toys and sweets and of course, Christmas lunch. This was a great ritual, starting off with Sherry, followed by Turkey and trimmings, the ritualistic carving (always done by the male head of the household) and Christmas pudding in which would be hidden tiny, silver sixpences. The Port and Stilton cheese, mince pies and Christmas crackers (filled with useless little objects like micro-sized tape measures and fluorescent key chains) would complete the day followed by massive indigestion and Turkey sandwiches for several weeks after.

The Turkey, for some unknown reason, is still the centre-piece on British tables. It is a stupid, highly strung bird (literally) which , if cooked badly, can taste like a cross between blotting paper and boiled string. However, reaching into my books on British culinary history, it seems that the factors determining why the Turkey is the all time British favourite are purely practical. It is a large bird which means it will feed the whole family and the ratio of its meat to bones makes it more affordable than the much tastier but more expensive goose, leg of ham, duck, suckling pig or game.

The Americans eat turkey only at Thanksgiving. They prefer Virginia and Kentucky smoked hams at Christmas. Virginia hams come from the razorback breed of hog which are fed on peanuts and peaches! The hams are cured over hickory and apple wood fires and kept in old fashioned smokehouses until ready. Kentucky hams (Hampshire hogs) are fed freely on beans, acorns and clover. They are first dry salted, then smoked over hickory and apple wood and finally hung to age for at least a year. Turkey is popular today (both as meat and as sausages, fillets and so on) because it is lean and low in cholesterol.

Interestingly, before the days of the turkey, the great British delicacy was Boar's head at Christmas. However this was stopped because the ritual killing of the animal was a remnant of an earlier, pre-Christian rite in which a human being, a mock king was sacrificed! The taste factor, with its squishy and crunchy bits, was another reason for the demise of the habit.

But the best part about the turkey has to be the add-ons: the gravy made with the meat juices, the bread sauce, the Brussels sprouts and sausages and the stuffing. I personally think the stuffing is the best part and would advise you (if you are a little unorthodox) to actually shove a lemon, orange, apple, some herbs, onion and garlic into the cavity of the bird (which keeps it more moist than a bread based stuffing) and cook the stuffing on the side.

Almost everything except chocolate bars, ice cream and candy can be used to stuff a turkey. Tradition dictates that the stuffing should be based on something starchy like bread (but rice, chestnuts, walnuts or potatoes are all acceptable), bound with egg and incorporating something meaty (bacon, sausage, ham) or mushrooms or oysters (the best of all), something aromatic (herbs like thyme and sage and onions and garlic) and something crunchy like walnuts, celery or pistachios.

I must say a few words in favour of the turkey. It is an extremely versatile creature. It is an excellent low cholesterol lean meat. But you have to "tart" it up with spices or exotic sauces. The Chinese have devised recipes for turkey steaks using Oriental flavourings and cooking techniques. The Mexican national dish Mole Poblano is a delicious concoction using this Aztec bird smothered in a sauce of bitter chocolate, chillies, coriander, cinnamon and anise. In fact, because of the disparity between cooking times for the white meat (breast) and dark meat (legs and thighs) , cooking a whole turkey the traditional way is not the ideal way to go about it.

The way to get the best out of the bird is to amputate the legs and thighs and cook them at the same time but by the side of the breast and back, not attached to them. Alternatively, you can just cook the breast and carve it up into slices served with all the traditional accompaniments. Make drums of heaven out of the wings by pulling the flesh down on one side and save the legs and thighs to grill or roast with a more spicy, devilish sauce to which the dark meat is more suited.

Food

FOR . . . THE FIT MAN

4

FOREWORD

Most young people today are aware of fitness. Some take to the gym with gusto, others diet like devils. It just shows that health and diets are being taken seriously. This suits me fine. It is a path I have been following for a while – trying to create healthy recipes which don't compromise on taste. Salads and soups are an obvious start. They are easy to make, look great and taste wonderful. Snacking is always a problem area for me. After a whole day of being "good", I often end up gorging on a brownie at night. Completely useless. So, I've come up with a range of healthy sandwiches and wraps for smart snacking. And remember, there is a big difference between eating "healthy" and "low–fat". Although eating healthy is correct in the long run, it doesn't necessarily mean you will lose masses of weight immediately. And remember, low-fat does not mean "low-carb", Excessive carbs, especially the "bad" ones - white sugar, white flour, rice, potatos and pasta definetely make you "bulk".

METROSEXUAL MAN

GAZPACHO / WARM THAI-STYLE CHICKEN SALAD / SOM TAM / VICHYSSOISE / MEXICAN CORN WITH SALSA / LEAN BAINGAN KA BHARTHA

GAZPACHO

COLD TOMATO AND PEPPER SOUP

Serves 6

INGREDIENTS

½ kg ripe tomatoes, dunked in hot water for a few minutes, peeled
1 large cucumber, peeled
1 green capsicum seeded
1 spicy chilli like a jalapeño pepper, seeded
3 large cloves of garlic
½ jar Karen Anand's spicy Mexican salsa
3 slices bread
1 glass dry red wine
2 tbsps olive oil
½ litre tomato juice
salt and pepper to taste

METHOD

Chop the first five ingredients together in a food processor. Soak the bread in the wine and oil for half an hour until all the wine is absorbed. Mix with your hands. Put this along with all the other ingredients into the blender. Blend it until absolutely smooth or leave it slightly coarse according to your taste. Chill for at least two hours before serving.

Add ice cubes and put into little bowls with garnishes like fried croutons, chopped spring onions, chopped cucumber and chopped chilli around the soup.

KITCHEN ESSENTIALS

Food processor
Mixing bowl
Blender
Soup bowls

TIP

Can be served as a soup or a juice or spiked with vodka.

WARM THAI-STYLE CHICKEN SALAD

Serves 4

INGREDIENTS

For the chicken and marinade

3 whole chicken breast pieces
¼ cup fresh lime juice
2 tbsps fish sauce
2 cloves garlic, crushed
1 tbsp brown sugar or jaggery
2 tbsps finely chopped fresh coriander

Dressing

1 small red chilli, finely chopped
1 clove garlic, finely chopped
3 tbsps extra virgin olive oil
juice of 2 limes
2 tbsps Karen Anand's oriental stir-fry sauce

For the salad base

1 red bell pepper, remove seeds and membrane
2 carrots
1 cucumber
6 green spring onions, sliced
1 cup loosely packed fresh coriander sprigs
1 cup Thai basil (optional)
3 tbsps toasted sesame seeds
3 tbsps oriental sesame oil

METHOD

Remove skin and debone the chicken breasts. You should have 6 chicken fillets, two from each breast piece. Flatten the chicken fillets slightly and cut each lengthwise into two. Combine all of the marinade ingredients in a bowl and mix well. Add the chicken and toss to coat. Set aside, covered with cling film and refrigerate overnight or at room temperature for two hours.

Combine all the dressing ingredients in a small bowl and whisk until well combined. Cut the red bell pepper, carrot and cucumber into juliennes (long strips) and arrange on a large serving platter along with the spring onions.

Heat the sesame oil in a wok or frying pan until smoking. Fry the chicken until cooked through, about 6 minutes turning once. Remove and cut each piece into 4 at a slant. Place on the vegetable platter. Drizzle the dressing and sprinkle with the toasted sesame seeds,Thai basil and coriander sprigs. Serve immediately while the chicken is still warm.

KITCHEN ESSENTIALS

Food processor
Frying pans
Mixing bowl
Serving platter

TIP

Cutting into juliennes can be tedious to say the least. The best and most efficient way to achieve this I have found, is to use a food processor with a varying grating attachment. The blades are so sharp that they slice and grate vegetables in seconds without creating a watery mess.

SOM TAM

THAI GREEN PAPAYA SALAD

Serves 4-6

INGREDIENTS

300 gms unripe green papaya, peeled
7 green bird's eye chillies (or 4 hot green chillies)
6 cherry tomatoes, quartered, or one large tomato, cut into slices
5 cloves garlic
2 tbsps unsalted roasted peanuts
1 tbsp dried shrimps
3 tbsps lime juice
1 tbsp chopped jaggery
1 tbsp fish sauce
sprigs of basil to garnish

METHOD

Shred the papaya into juliennes using the shredder blade of the food processor (doing it by hand is possible but requires a special julienne cutter and is a tedious process with a knife). Remove. Take the chillies, garlic and peanuts. Chop roughly in the food processor or in a mortar and pestle.

Remove and mix with the raw papaya. Pound slightly to mix in the flavours. Stir in the dried shrimps and tomato, mix well. Make a paste of the jaggery, fish sauce and lime juice. Add to the papaya mixture. Serve at room temperature garnished with sprigs of basil.

KITCHEN ESSENTIALS
Food processor
Mixing bowls
Plate or bowl to serve

TIP
Spiking up salads with Thai ingredients is a great way to tempt people to eat them. Palm sugar is actually much darker and has a more intense flavour than normal jaggery but jaggery is a fair substitute.
Vegetarian version Replace the fish sauce and shrimps with sea salt.

VICHYSSOISE

COLD LEEK AND POTATO SOUP
Serves 4-6

INGREDIENTS
2 cups leeks, sliced fine or 8 spring onions
1 tbsp butter
1 large potato, peeled and sliced
6 cups vegetable stock
200 gms tofu, cubed
powdered roasted cumin / cumin dust

METHOD
Melt the butter and fry the leeks until soft, but not browned. Add potatoes and stock. Bring to the boil, lower heat and simmer for about half an hour. Add the tofu. Blend the soup until smooth.
Chill thoroughly in the fridge. Serve with roasted cumin.
Can also be served hot.

KITCHEN ESSENTIALS
Saucepan
Blender
Serving bowls

TIP
Leeks have to be sliced first and then rinsed several times in water.

MEXICAN CORN WITH SALSA
Serves 4

INGREDIENTS
2 cups fresh American sweetcorn kernels
1 cup red and green pepper (capsicums), chopped
1 white onion chopped fine
2 tbsps jalapeños, chopped fine
2 tbsps olive oil
6 black olives
freshly ground pepper
½ cup Karen Anand's spicy Mexican salsa
avocado slices (optional)
coriander sprigs
black salt

METHOD
Boil the corn in salted water until tender (approx 5 mins). Drain.
In a frying pan, heat the olive oil and fry the onions for a couple of minutes only. They should still be a little crunchy. Add the corn and toss once. Then add the green and red peppers. Stir once and remove from heat. Add pepper and black salt. Stir this in while the corn is still warm. Empty into a bowl, Add the olives and jalapeños. Pour on the Mexican salsa. Decorate with sliced avocado and coriander sprigs. Serve at room temperature.

KITCHEN ESSENTIALS
Handi
Frying pan
Salad bowl

TIP
Fresh American corn is now available in packets and on the cob. If you can't find it use tinned 'Green Giant Corn.'

LEAN BAINGAN KA BHARTHA

Serves 4-6

INGREDIENTS

2 large aubergines, approx. 750 gms
1 tsp cumin seeds, roasted
1 tbsp finely grated ginger
1 tbsp finely chopped garlic
1 large onion, finely chopped
4 tomatoes, skinned and chopped
3 green chillies, finely chopped
2 tbsps yoghurt, whipped
1 cup fresh coriander, freshly chopped
4 tbsps olive oil
salt to taste

METHOD

Make a few slits in the aubergines and roast each over a medium gas flame until the skin has charred all over. Cool. Discard the skin and mash the flesh with the back of a fork.
Heat the olive oil and fry the onion for two minutes until soft but not brown. Add the cumin seeds, ginger and garlic. Cook for just a minute. Add the aubergines and the tomatoes, Cook for five or six minutes until thick. Take off the gas and add the green chillies, whipped yoghurt and fresh coriander. Stir well. Serve hot with tandoori rotis or at room temperature as a dip.

KITCHEN ESSENTIALS

Frying pan
Serving dish

TIP

Baingan can be roasted in a hot oven for about 20 minutes, until the skin starts darkening and the flesh is soft. The flame method is more laborious but the flavour is better.

SUNDAY BRUNCH

SPINACH QUICHE / CARROT, PEANUT AND RAISIN SALAD / BROCCOLI MOUSSE / FRUIT SALAD WITH MINT AND PRESERVED GINGER / KIWI AND LIME PIE (MOCKTAIL)

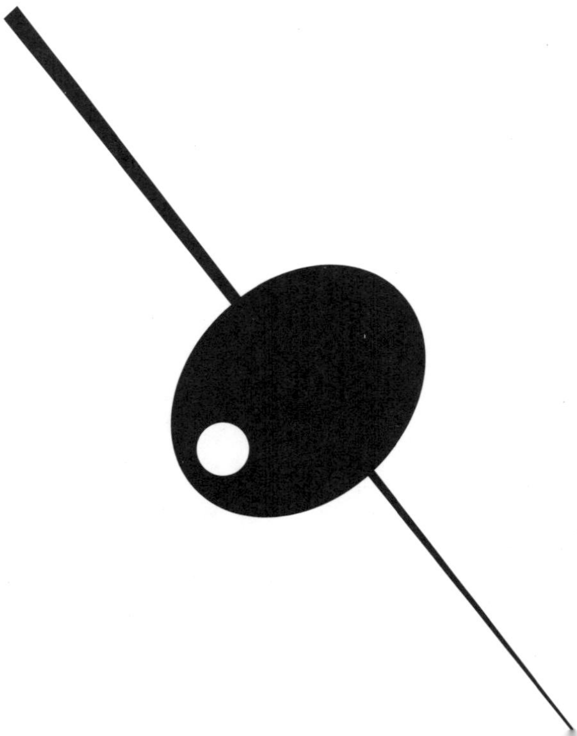

SPINACH QUICHE
Serves 6

INGREDIENTS
Shortcrust pastry
200 gms whole wheat flour (atta)
100 gms butter, chilled, cut into cubes
½ cup water
½ tsp salt

Filling
3 eggs
200 ml cream
50 ml milk
pinch of mixed herbs
pinch of salt
pinch of crushed black pepper
1 cup cheddar cheese, grated
1 cup spinach which has been blanched, drained and chopped

METHOD
Sift the flour and salt. Add butter. Using only the tips of your fingers, rub the flour and butter together to form light crumbs. When you have a moist, sand-like texture, add the water and knead lightly.
Form into a ball and leave the pastry to relax for at least half an hour in a cool place or wrap in cling film and leave in the fridge.
Your pastry will be perfect and is guaranteed not to shrink if you follow these basic instructions: Roll the pastry to ¼" thick to line an 8" pastry case/flan dish. Bake blind for 10 minutes. Mix together the eggs, cream, milk, herbs, salt and pepper. Place the spinach at the bottom of the dish and pour on the egg mixture. Top with grated cheese and bake in a preheated moderate oven for 20 minutes or until golden. Serve warm or at room temperature.

KITCHEN ESSENTIALS
Oven
Mixing bowls
Pastry dish
Plate to serve

TIP
There is no need to knead the dough for more than a few minutes. If you do, you will find that the butter starts melting and your dough will become very greasy.

CARROT, PEANUT AND RAISIN SALAD

Serves 4

INGREDIENTS

500 gms juicy carrots, peeled and cut into juliennes
½ cup roasted peanuts, roughly chopped
½ cup raisins
¼ cup coriander leaves
2 tbsps sesame seeds, roasted

DRESSING

½ cup orange juice
¼ cup lime juice
2 cloves garlic, crushed
1 tsp honey
1 tsp whole cumin, roasted
1 tbsp Karen Anand's chunky orange marmalade
salt and pepper to taste

METHOD

Mix all the dressing ingredients first. Steam the carrots for a couple of minutes only. They should still be very crunchy and bright orange in colour. Refresh them with ice or put them in the fridge to cool. Soak the raisins in warm water for a few minutes. Drain.

Mix all the salad ingredients with the dressing. It is not essential but preferable that the salad is chilled. If the carrots absorb all the dressing while chilling, make some more dressing and add just before serving.

KITCHEN ESSENTIALS

Mixing bowls
Food processor
Salad bowl

TIP

In winter when the carrots are really fresh, you do not need to steam them.

BROCCOLI MOUSSE
Serves 6

INGREDIENTS
½ kg broccoli (choose small florets with tender stems)
300 gms cream cheese
100 gms cheese spread
½ cup cream
1 tbsp garlic
1 tbsp lime juice
2 tbsps gelatine
1 red pepper (Capsicum) roasted and cut into strips
1 cup stock
salt and pepper to taste

METHOD
Steam the broccoli in a colander over boiling water until tender. Reserve a few florets. Refresh them with ice. Chop up all the rest, in a food processor or by hand.
Soak the gelatine in the lime juice and half the stock for a few minutes. Heat gently in a microwave or over hot water until all the gelatine is absorbed and you get a thick, runny liquid.
Put all the ingredients, except the red pepper, through a blender in batches. You can blend it as rough or as smooth as you like. Add the red pepper. Grease a jelly mould with a little oil and pour in the mixture. Chill for two hours.
To serve, unmould the mousse and decorate with the remaining broccoli.

KITCHEN ESSENTIALS
Bowl to soak
Steamer or handi with sieve
Food processor
Jelly mould
Serving plate

TIP
The mousse is delicious with whole-wheat bread or melba toast. It can also be made in advance and stored in either the fridge or freezer.

FRUIT SALAD WITH MINT AND PRESERVED GINGER

Serves 4-6

INGREDIENTS

1 small green/orange melon, peeled, seeded and cut into 2 inch cubes
2 cups grapes (green or black), preferably seedless
2 cups fresh pineapple, cleaned and cut into 2 inch cubes
1 cup fresh mint leaves
2 tbsps ginger, finely chopped
1½ cups water
4 tbsps honey
juice of 1 lime

METHOD

Put the ginger, lime juice, honey and water into a saucepan. Bring to a boil and simmer uncovered until the ginger is soft and the syrup has thickened (about 15-20 minutes). The syrup should have reduced by half. Cool and refrigerate.

Add a few tablespoons of this to any fruit salad. The ginger brings out the delicate flavour and sweetness of melon and pineapple. It is also good with fresh figs and oranges. Pour over the fruit and serve chilled.

KITCHEN ESSENTIALS

Saucepan
Salad bowls

TIP

Ginger syrup can be made in advance especially in the monsoon when it is tender and will last in sugar syrup for a year.

Any fruit can be used but those high in water content like any kind of melon, strawberry and grapes are better. Avoid bananas and apples.

KIWI AND LIME PIE (MOCKTAIL)
Serves 1

INGREDIENTS
juice of two limes
2 Marie biscuits
½ kiwi fruit
2 tbsps sugar syrup
¾ cup milk
1 scoop vanilla ice cream
ice
½ tsp lime rind

METHOD
Crumble the biscuits to fine powder. In a blender add all the ingredients except the biscuit and blend to a smooth milk shake consistency. Serve in a tall glass with the lime rind, kiwi slices and biscuit crumbs.

KITCHEN ESSENTIALS
Blender
Tall glasses

TIP
Never blend a drink for more than seven seconds.

SALADS AND CHAATS

THAI BEEF SALAD / CHICKEN IN MANGO MAYONNAISE / THREE BEAN CHAAT / PINEAPPLE AND COTTAGE CHEESE CHAAT / CITRUS SALAD

FOREWORD

Say "Salads" and you are guaranteed a real mixed bunch of reactions. You'll get some people who say politely, "No thank you, I'm not a rabbit" to the nervous, energetic, workout fiend, crying for more. You cannot deny, though, that salads have come a long way since the days of glutinous mayonnaise coleslaw and soggy lettuce. With exposure and health awareness has also come availability of ingredients and the willingness to experiment with salads as a meal, not just some apology on the side. There are of course Indian salads too – delicious, crunchy koshimbirs, cooling raithas, tangy chaats and South Indian delights made with spicy temperings. But they somehow have still not caught on as main courses and dutifully remain on the side of the banana leaf or thali or eaten as a snack. Nowadays, when we talk about salads, we usually mean voluptuous, sexy ones. The kind that are tossed in exotic dressings with dressed with even more exotic raw vegetables.

For the weak hearted, salads are still not enough to satisfy the soul. They need something more substantial – a one stop, clean, wholesome solution to get them through the day. The sandwich is the perfect answer. Stuffed to the brim with a variety of fillings, enclosed in a variety of breads – this is the modern answer to lunch, whether you opt for a sinful, creamy cheesy one, laden with mayonnaise or a light, healthy, low calorie version.

SALAD - TIPS

ASPARAGUS – Asparagus has a very delicate, nutty flavour. It is perfect steamed with a tempering of sesame seeds (til), dry red chilli broken into pieces and garlic or simply steamed and tossed into salads. It also lends itself well to creamy dressings and cheesy sauces.

BROCCOLI – is a member of the cauliflower and cabbage family and actually looks like green cauliflower but has a more delicate flavour. It is usually very tender and therefore takes little time to cook. Broccoli is excellent steamed with a tempering of garlic and a dash of oyster or soya sauce or steamed and tossed cold with a creamy, cheesy dressing. Broccoli must always be wrapped tightly in cling film and stored in the fridge. If left open, it will turn yellow.

RED & YELLOW PEPPER / BELL PEPPERS – look just like our green capsicum but have a thicker, crisp, firm flesh and a sweeter flavour. Raw peppers are excellent in salads.

CELERY - In India, celery has a much stronger flavour and tends to be green and woody. It is perfect chopped fine in salads, to flavor soups and stews and stir-fries. Celery abroad is thick and white with a milder flavour. In India use only the stalks. Remove and discard the leaves and the outer stringy part of the stalks.

LETTUCE - Is a favourite with weight watchers, because of its low calorie content. There are several varieties of lettuce ranging from the sweet, crisp iceberg to the curly bitter endive and the robust, hardy cos or romaine. Columbus took lettuce to the New World and today it is the most popular salad plant in the world.

Choose crisp, fresh, firm lettuce, heavy for their size. Avoid any damp or brown edged leaves and soft white cores. Under a cold running tap wash well then drain or dry by shaking in a clean dry tea towel or a salad spinner.

Always remember to refresh salad ingredients, whether raw or steamed in plenty of iced water, to retain their freshness and crispness. Drain well and pat dry before serving.

THAI BEEF SALAD

Serves 6

INGREDIENTS

500 gms beef fillet (undercut), cut into steaks
1 tbsp olive oil
2 cups mixed lettuce leaves
1 cup cherry tomatoes
2 cucumbers, peeled and chopped
2 onions, sliced
3 tbsps fresh mint leaves

DRESSING

1 stalk (white part only) fresh lemon grass, chopped (optional) or
1 tsp finely grated lime rind
3 tbsps fresh coriander leaves
1 tbsp jaggery
2 tbsps lime juice
1 tbsp light soya sauce
4 tbsps Thai fish sauce
2 tbsps sweet chilli sauce

METHOD

Heat the oil in a frying pan over high heat until hot. Add beef and cook for one or two minutes on each side or until cooked to your liking. Set aside to cool. Arrange lettuce, tomatoes, cucumber, onions and mint attractively on a serving platter.

To make dressing, place lemon grass or lime rind, coriander, jaggery, lime juice, soy, chilli and fish sauces in a bowl. Mix to combine. Slice beef thinly and arrange on salad, then drizzle with dressing and serve.

KITCHEN ESSENTIALS

Frying pan
Mixing bowl
Serving platter

TIP

For best results char grill the beef just before you are making the salad and toss into the salad while still warm.

CHICKEN IN MANGO MAYONNAISE

Serves 4-6

INGREDIENTS

500 gms chicken breast (boneless), roasted and cut into 1 inch pieces
1 cup Karen Anand's mayonnaise
3 fresh mangoes, cut into cubes (discard seed)
½ cup mango juice
1 tsp curry powder
2 large capsicums (green, red), cut into 1 inch pieces
10 no. red radish, cut into rounds
1 tin water chestnuts, cut into rounds (optional)
or 100 gms fresh water chestnuts (singhada)

METHOD

Mix the mayonnaise with the mango pieces and the curry powder. Add the mango juice. Reserve a few good slices of radish for garnish. Mix the rest of the ingredients with the dressing and arrange on a platter. Garnish with red radish.

KITCHEN ESSENTIALS

Mixing bowl
Serving platter

TIP

Fresh Alphonso mango is ideal for this recipe. However when they are not in season, the salad can still be made with tinned mangoes so long as you drain all the sugar syrup.

THREE BEAN CHAAT

Serves 4-6

INGREDIENTS

½ cup rajma
½ cup black eyed beans
½ cup chickpeas
1 tbsp chaat masala
4 tbsps lime juice
½ cup fresh coriander
2 onions, finely chopped
½ cup fresh pomegranate seeds

METHOD

Soak the rajma, beans and peas separately overnight. Drain, wash in several changes of water and boil each separately with salt. You will get approximately double the quantity when cooked. Cool and drain. Place all the drained beans in a bowl. Add the remaining ingredients and toss.

KITCHEN ESSENTIALS

Bowls to soak
Handi
Serving bowl

TIP

Beans when cooked will last upto a week in the fridge without water.

PINEAPPLE AND COTTAGE CHEESE CHAAT

Serves 6

INGREDIENTS

200 gms paneer cut into ½ inch cubes
1 fresh pineapple, cut into 1 inch cubes
1 tsp chaat masala
½ cup mint chopped fine
1 tbsp honey
1 tbsp lime juice
sprigs of mint for garnish

METHOD

Toss the pineapple cubes with the chaat masala, honey, mint, paneer and lime juice. Serve in the pineapple shell and garnish with sprigs of fresh mint.

KITCHEN ESSENTIALS

Mixing bowl
Serving bowl / Pineapple shell

TIP

Cut a pineapple with the green bush into 2 lengthways. Carefully scoop out all the flesh cutting around the outer edge with a sharp knife leaving about ½ inch from the sides and bottom.

CITRUS SALAD
Serves 4-6

INGREDIENTS
a big bowl of mixed lettuce
8-10 pieces of sun-dried tomatoes
6 black olives
½ cup Parmesan cheese shavings
½ cup of balsamic and orange dressing
8-10 spears asparagus, steamed

FOR THE BALSAMIC AND ORANGE DRESSING
4 tbsps olive oil
2 tbsps balsamic vinegar
½ tsp salt
½ tsp black pepper
1½ tbsp Karen Anand's chunky orange marmalade
½ tsp chopped garlic

METHOD
Wash and dry the lettuce completely. Throw it into a salad bowl with all the salad ingredients, except the cheese. Whisk all the ingredients for the dressing. Pour over the salad. Toss and serve. Just before serving, sprinkle with the cheese shavings.

KITCHEN ESSENTIALS
Mixing bowl
Salad bowl

TIP
To make cheese shavings, the easiest way is to use a potato peeler. Sun-dried tomatoes are available ready to eat in oil or dried. If using the latter, soak in warm water for ten minutes. Drain and then use / eat.

SANDWICHES AND SNACKS

ROASTED VEGETABLES WITH SUN-DRIED TOMATO PESTO CROSTINI / PITA POCKETS WITH GREEK SALAD / MIDDLE EASTERN CHICKEN PARCELS / HOT BEEF ROLLS / MINI HAMBURGERS / PARTY MINI HOT DOGS / TANGY TUNA SANDWICH / EGG MAYONNAISE BAGUETTES

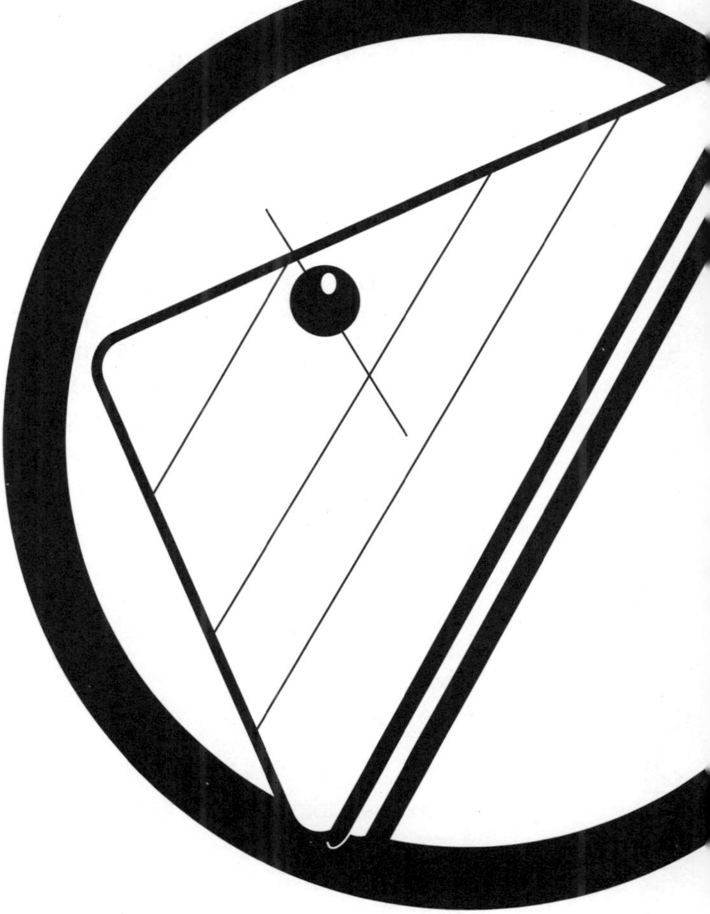

ROASTED VEGETABLES WITH SUN-DRIED TOMATO PESTO CROSTINI

Makes 12

INGREDIENTS

1 courgette, cut into rounds
1 red pepper, sliced
1 yellow pepper, sliced
3 cloves garlic, crushed
¼ cup olive oil
2 tbsps balsamic vinegar
1 tsp dry herbs
salt and pepper
sliced crusty bread

For the sun-dried tomato pesto

8 pieces sun-dried tomatoes
2 large cloves garlic
4-5 leaves fresh basil or ½ tsp dried basil
4 tbsps olive brine
2 tbsps olive oil

METHOD

Mix the vegetables with all the ingredients except the bread and bake in a preheated oven for 20 minutes. Cool. Put all the pesto ingredients in the small grinder jar of a mixer. Grind till completely smooth. This can be stored in the fridge for upto two weeks. Spread pesto onto slices of crusty bread. Pile on the roasted vegetables and serve. Can be garnished with a sprig of fresh thyme or rosemary.

KITCHEN ESSENTIALS

OTG
Mixer grinder
Oven-proof dish
Mixing bowl
Plate to serve

TIP

If sun-dried tomatoes are in a packet, reconstitute them in luke warm water for ten minutes before using. If they are already in oil, use directly, drained. When using olives from a jar, do not throw out the salty water. This comes in very handy as a vegetarian stock which can be added to any sauce or dressing.

PITA POCKETS WITH GREEK SALAD

Makes 12

INGREDIENTS

6 medium pita breads, halved
3 ripe tomatoes cut into 1 inch cubes
1cucumber, peeled, split in half, roughly cubed
1green pepper, seeded and roughly cubed
1 white onion, thinly sliced in rings
150 gms feta cheese, cubed
12 black olives
1 tbsp parsley, chopped
1 cup garlic yoghurt dressing

METHOD

Mix all the above ingredients together (except the pita bread). Take care not to smash the feta cheese.

DRESSING

¾ cup whipped yoghurt
1 tsp garlic, crushed
¼ tsp salt
1 tsp honey
1 tbsp cream

METHOD

Place the dressing ingredients in a bowl and whisk.

SANDWICH METHOD

Gently warm the pita breads and stuff with some salad.
Pour on a spoonful of garlic yoghurt dressing.

KITCHEN ESSENTIALS

Mixing bowls
Plate to serve

MIDDLE EASTERN CHICKEN PARCELS

Makes 12

INGREDIENTS
4 boneless chicken breasts
sunflower oil for frying

For marinade
4 cloves garlic, crushed
1 tbsp lime juice
1 tsp cumin seeds, roasted and crushed
1 tsp freshly ground black pepper
2 tbsps extra virgin olive oil
salt

To serve
roomali roti
250 gms hummus* or tahini
harissa or chilli sauce
6 spring onion greens, cut into strips, blanched in hot water

METHOD
Mix the marinade ingredients together and rub over the chicken. Marinate for 20 minutes or overnight to develop the flavours. To cook the chicken, heat oil in a pan, add the drained chicken breast and sauté gently on each side until tender for about 15 minutes. To assemble, heat the roomali briefly, then put a heaped teaspoon of hummus in the middle, some sliced chicken and a dab of chilli sauce. Roll up the roomali into a square parcel, folding over each end to enclose the filling. Tie up with spring onion greens.

KITCHEN ESSENTIALS
Mixing bowl
Frying pan
Plate to serve

TIP
For an alternative kathi kebab, roll into a wrap, and cut into four.
* See page 42.

HOT BEEF ROLLS
Makes 8 large rolls

INGREDIENTS
½ kg beef fillet (undercut)
4 tbsps olive oil
8 bread rolls
butter (optional)
salad leaves
sea salt
black pepper, crushed
Karen Anand's classic mayonnaise

METHOD
To roast the beef, heat a roasting tin on top of a stove and add the olive oil and swirl to coat the surface. Sprinkle the fillet with sea salt and crushed pepper. Place the whole fillet of beef on the tin and fry on a high heat on all sides until browned for about 5 minutes. Preheat the oven to the maximum and put the ovenproof dish into the oven and roast for 15-20 minutes. Remove from the oven and set aside. Cool, then cut into strips suitable for stuffing the roll. Cut the rolls in half. Smear butter, if using. Put a pinch of salad leaves into the pocket, 2-3 strips of roast beef and top with a teaspoon of either plain or spiced mayonnaise.

KITCHEN ESSENTIALS
Oven
Roasting tin
Plate to serve

TIP
For wasabi mayonnaise, add one teaspoon of prepared wasabi to half a cup of mayonnaise. For mustard mayonnaise use one teaspoon of Karen Anand's wholegrain mustard to one-fourth cup of mayonnaise.

MINI HAMBURGERS

Makes 12 mini or 6 normal ones

INGREDIENTS

12 burger buns
Karen Anand's barbecue sauce
salad leaves
10 cherry tomatoes, sliced
4 pickled onions, sliced
12 gherkins

FOR THE HAMBURGER PATTIES

500 gms minced beef
1 onion, finely chopped
3 cloves garlic, crushed
1 red chilli, seeded and finely chopped
1 egg, beaten
a pinch of freshly ground nutmeg
½ cup white breadcrumbs
salt and pepper
peanut oil, for frying

METHOD

Put all the patty ingredients except the oil into a bowl and mix well. Take one heaped tablespoon of the mixture and shape into a round flat patty. Repeat until all the mixture is used. Heat oil in a frying pan until hot and shallow fry the patties for 2-3 minutes, turning half way, until cooked through. Remove from the pan and drain on kitchen paper.

Preheat the buns, then split, leaving one side attached if possible. Put a dot of barbecue sauce or chilli sauce into each bun, then a salad leaf, a patty, tomato and onion ring. Close the bun and secure with a cocktail stick and a baby gherkin.

KITCHEN ESSENTIALS

Mixing bowl
Frying pan
Plate to serve

TIP

For white breadcrumbs, leave ordinary white bread or rolls on a window sill to dry completely for at least two days. Break into pieces and grind in the small grinder of the mixer until you get a sandy consistency.

PARTY MINI HOT DOGS

Makes 12 mini or 6 normal ones

INGREDIENTS

12 mini hot dog rolls
12 mini sausages or chicken frankfurters
1 tbsp olive oil
crispy fried onions (optional)
Karen Anand's wholegrain mustard

METHOD

Heat oil in a frying pan and fry the sausages until cooked through. Take the sausages or frankfurters and place into slit hot dog rolls. You may need to cut them into half depending on the size of your rolls. Place some crispy fried onions and mustard or tomato ketchup on top of each sausage, and serve.

KITCHEN ESSENTIALS

Frying pan
Plate to serve

TIP

To prepare the frankfurters, bring a large saucepan of water to the boil, then remove from heat. Put all the frankfurters into the saucepan for about three minutes until heated through, remove with a slotted spoon.

TANGY TUNA SANDWICH

Makes 6 hefty brown bread sandwiches

INGREDIENTS

1 loaf sliced brown bread
1 tin tuna drained of all oil
½ jar Karen Anand's garlic mayonnaise
2 small gherkins, chopped
few drops of Tabasco
lettuce for garnish

METHOD

Put the tuna into a bowl with the garlic mayonnaise and smash with a fork till you get a paste like consistency. Add gherkins and as much Tabasco as you like. Place a large dollop on a slice of brown bread. Place a leaf of lettuce on top and cover with the second slice. Cut the bread edges off if you want something fancy. Otherwise just cut the sandwich into two diagonally.

KITCHEN ESSENTIALS

Mixing bowl
Plate to serve

TIP

Lakshwadeep tinned tuna is the best white tuna available in India. I would advise you to stock up when you see this in your super market since supplies are not regular.

EGG MAYONNAISE BAGUETTES

Makes 4 sandwiches

INGREDIENTS

4 hard-boiled eggs, chopped fine
½ jar of Karen Anand's classic mayonnaise
½ cup spring onion greens, chopped
French loaf (baguette)

METHOD

Place the hard boiled eggs in a bowl. Mix in the mayonnaise untill smooth. Add the spring onion greens. Cut the French loaf into four and slice horizontally. Remove a little of the bread if necessary and stuff each with a generous helping of the filling.

KITCHEN ESSENTIALS

Mixing bowls
Plate to serve

TIP

For a quick gas-saving technique, place eggs in cold water on the gas. Turn the gas on. As soon as the water begins to boil, turn the gas off and cover with a tight lid for 10 minutes.

FOREWORD

There are times when I simply don't want to step out of the house. I don't want to bathe. I convince myself that I'm coming down with something nasty. It's the dreaded "don't do anything" diseases that, at times, we all suffer from. Nothing will console me more than a bowl of delicious, steaming, soup or a spicy stew.

Then there are times when there's no money around to order anything fancy. Another scenario: you've been getting home late from work all week and have been eating out a lot. On Sunday you discover that you have a couple of dead tomatoes in the fridge, potatoes with green things growing out, three containers of half eaten cheese and a loaf of dry bread.

And you feel like cooking. Not impossible. Let's take a trek to the kitchen and see what we can do. I know that my creativity is at its peak when I have little or nothing to work with.

Food

FOR . . .WHEN THE GOING IS TOUGH

5

HEALING THE SOUL

SAIGON CHICKEN SOUP / RASAM /
KERALA VEGETABLE STEW / THAI FRIED RICE

SAIGON CHICKEN SOUP

Serves 4-6

INGREDIENTS

1 litre chicken stock
2 chicken breast fillets, trimmed
4 black peppercorns
1 inch piece of ginger, thinly sliced
1 clove garlic, crushed
1 small onion, thinly sliced
¼ cup crisp fried onions, plus extra, to serve
1 tbsp fish sauce
3 tsps light soya sauce
100 gms dried rice noodles
6 prawns, shelled and cleaned, leaving tails intact
¼ cup bean sprouts, tailed
2 tbsps mint leaves
2 tbsps coriander leaves, chopped
sliced green onions, sliced red chillies, sprigs of coriander, lime wedges to serve

METHOD

Combine chicken stock, peppercorns, ginger, garlic, onion, crisp fried onions, fish sauce and soya sauce in a large saucepan and bring to the boil, then simmer gently over moderately low heat for 5 minutes. Add chicken and gently simmer for 12-15 minutes or until cooked through. Remove chicken, cool slightly, then slice and set aside.

Strain stock, discarding solids, then return stock to a clean saucepan, season to taste and bring to a simmer. Soak noodles in warm water for 10 minutes, then drain well. Divide noodles in four bowls. Add prawns to simmering stock and cook for 2-3 minutes or until just cooked, then, using a slotted spoon, place 3 prawns and a few chicken slices in a bowl.

Top with bean sprouts, mint and coriander, then ladle over stock. Serve immediately topped with green onions red chillies, sprigs of coriander and extra crisp fried shallots, with lime wedges on the side.

KITCHEN ESSENTIALS

Saucepans
Soup bowls

TIP

For a tangy spicy version of this soup add two crushed green or red chillies and one tablespoon of lime juice to the chicken stock while boiling.

RASAM

Serves 4-6

INGREDIENTS

½ kg large ripe tomatoes, chopped
1tbsp tamarind pulp
¼ cup tuvar dal
1 large onion, sliced
3 cloves of garlic, crushed
1 tbsp pepper corns
8 coriander stalks
7½ cups water
¼ tsp mustard seeds (black)
¼ tsp fenugreek seeds
10 curry leaves
3 red chillies, broken
2-3 tbsps cooked rice (optional)
¼ cup coriander leaves (do not chop)
1 tbsp vegetable oil
salt

METHOD

Put all the ingredients except the coriander leaves, curry leaves, mustard, fenugreek and red chillies into a large pan. Bring to the boil and then simmer for 20 minutes to half an hour. Strain through a fine sieve. Season with salt if needed. Heat oil in a small pan. Throw in the curry leaves, mustard, fenugreek and red chillies. When the mustard crackles pour onto the rasam. Serve piping hot, garnished with the coriander leaves.

KITCHEN ESSENTIALS

Large handi
Tadka pan
Serving bowl

TIP

For a more substantial soup which can be a one course, quick lunch, use half a cup of dal and add to the rasam water as above. Add a few tablespoons of cooked rice to the soup.

KERALA VEGETABLE STEW

Serves 4-6

INGREDIENTS

4 tbsps vegetable oil
6 green cardamom pods, whole
6 cloves, whole
1 inch cinnamon stick
1 green chilli, slit in half lengthwise
2 tsps ginger, cut into julienne strips
½ cup onion, sliced
¾ cup peeled and diced carrots
1 cup peeled and diced potatoes
1½ tsp salt
1½ cups water
½ cup chopped French beans
1 cup cauliflower, cut into small florets
10-15 curry leaves
1 tsp black peppercorns, coarsely crushed
2 cups coconut milk

METHOD

In a medium-sized pan, heat oil and sauté the cardamom, cloves and cinnamon sticks for half a minute on medium heat. Add green chillies, ginger, onion and saute for two minutes.

Add carrots, potatoes, salt and water, cover pan with lid and cook for five minutes, stir in the French beans, cauliflower and the curry leaves and continue cooking for 8 minutes or until tender.

Add peppercorns and coconut milk and simmer for a minute on very low heat so that the coconut milk does not curdle, adjust salt as needed, and serve immediately.

KITCHEN ESSENTIALS

Large handi
Serving bowl

TIP

The original recipe uses coconut oil in which you fry onions and pour over stew like tadka. I find this unnecessarily heavy and certainly not the kind of food that puts you back on your feet!

THAI FRIED RICE

Serves 4-6

INGREDIENTS

3 tbsps vegetable oil
2 cloves garlic, finely chopped
1 medium-sized onion, finely chopped
150 gms any meat or chicken, cooked and diced
3 tbsps dried shrimp (soaked 5 mins, drained) optional
4 tbsps tomato ketchup
1 tsp sugar
pinch of salt
500 gms cooked rice
2 eggs, lightly beaten
1 tomato, diced
½ capsicum, chopped
fresh coriander leaves, to garnish

METHOD

Heat oil in a large wok over medium heat and sauté garlic and onion until garlic is golden. Add dried shrimp, meat pieces, tomato ketchup, sugar and salt. Stir-fry for about one minute and add rice and stir. Push rice to one side of wok, add a little more oil and pour in beaten egg.

Allow to set slightly, and then scramble. Stir egg through rice. And then add tomato and capsicum. Stir several times and remove from heat. Garnish with chopped coriander leaves.

KITCHEN APPLIANCES

Wok or large frying pan
Rice platter

TIP

Use left-over rice, not freshly cooked rice. For a vegetarian version, omit the shrimp and meat. There is no need to replace them with any vegetables.

LEFTOVERS

CHICKEN CROQUETTES / HAM QUICHE / CREAMY POTATO GRATIN / PANNA COTTA (ITALIAN BAKED CREAM)

CHICKEN CROQUETTES

Makes 8

INGREDIENTS

4 tbsps butter
½ cup plain flour (maida)
1 cup milk
1 roasted chicken breast chopped
1 clove garlic, finely chopped
1 egg, beaten
1 cup fresh white breadcrumbs
vegetable oil, for deep-frying
salt and ground black pepper
fresh parsley, to garnish
lime wedges, to serve

METHOD

For basic thick white sauce

Melt the butter in a small pan over a low heat.
Add the flour and cook gently, stirring constantly, for 1 minute.
Gradually add the milk, whisking constantly to make a smooth, very thick sauce.

METHOD

Mix the chicken with the sauce. Season with garlic, salt and pepper to taste. Leave to cool completely. Shape the mixture into eight even-sized sausages, then dip each in egg and then in the breadcrumbs. Deep-fry in hot oil for four minutes, until crisp and golden. Drain on kitchen paper and serve garnished with parsley and lime wedges.

KITCHEN ESSENTIALS

Sauce pan
Mixing bowl
Frying pan

TIP

To avoid the white sauce turning lumpy make sure you cook the butter and flour properly before adding the milk.

HAM QUICHE

Serves 6

INGREDIENTS

Shortcrust pastry

200 gms wheat flour (atta)
100 gms butter, chilled, cut into cubes
½ cup water
½ tsp salt

Filling

3 eggs
200 ml cream
50 ml milk
pinch of mixed herbs
pinch of salt
pinch of crushed black pepper
1 cup cheddar cheese, grated
1 cup ham, chopped

METHOD

Sift the flour and salt. Add butter. Using only the tips of your fingers, rub the flour and butter together to form light crumbs. When you have a moist, sand-like texture, add the water and knead lightly. Form into a ball and leave the pastry to relax for at least half an hour in a cool place or wrap in cling film and leave in the fridge. Your pastry will be perfect and is guaranteed not to shrink if you follow these basic instructions.

Roll the pastry to ¼" thick to line an 8" round pastry case/flan dish. Bake blind for 10 minutes. Mix together the eggs, cream, milk, herbs, salt and pepper. Place the ham at the bottom of the dish and pour on the egg mixture. Top with grated cheese and bake in a moderate oven for 20 minutes or until golden. Serve warm or at room temperature.

KITCHEN ESSENTIALS

OTG
Mixing bowls
Pastry dish
Plate to serve

TIP

Pastry has to be made in advance or kept in the fridge. Making it with wholewheat flour (atta) is much healthier than maida but it has a tendency to crack, so work fast !

CREAMY POTATO GRATIN

Serves 6

INGREDIENTS

5 large potatoes
500 ml milk
500 ml thick cream
1 whole onion, peeled and cut into four
2 cloves garlic, chopped
1 tbsp salt
50 gms butter

METHOD

Peel the potatoes and cut them into slices (approx. ½ inch thick) and put them into a large saucepan with the milk, cream, onion, garlic and salt. Bring to a boil and simmer until almost tender, but not dissolving into mush.

Use some of the butter to grease a large roasting tin or glass dish. Pour the almost sludgy milk and potato mixture into it. Dot with remaining butter and cook in a preheated oven for 15 minutes or until the potato is bubbly and browned on top. Remove it. Let it stand for 10 minutes and then serve.

KITCHEN ESSENTIALS

OTG
Sauce pan
Roasting tin or large glass dish
Serving plate

TIP

By cooking the potatoes first in a pan you are sure that the dish is going to be completely cooked and soft. You can do the pan-cooking well in advance and the quick blast in the oven while people are at the table. This is a wicked, fattening recipe from Nigella Lawson, but you'll find the bowl wiped clean!

PANNA COTTA

ITALIAN BAKED CREAM (DESSERT)

Serves 6

INGREDIENTS

1 tbsp gelatine
500 ml cream
¼ cup sugar
1 ½ tsp vanilla extract or essence
1 tbsp dark rum
Karen Anand's chunky orange marmalade or fresh fruit to decorate

METHOD

Soak the gelatine in a little cold water until soft. Heat gently in a microwave or over hot water until all the gelatine is absorbed and you get a thick, runny liquid. Leave aside to cool.

In a heavy-based saucepan, mix the cream with the sugar and vanilla essence. Bring to the boil. Take off the heat and add the gelatine and the rum. Stir well until the gelatine has dissolved. Pour into 4-5 small bowls. Put in the refrigerator to set. Decorate with chunky orange marmalade or fresh fruit.

KITCHEN ESSENTIALS

Bowl
Pan
Bowl to soak
Serving bowls

TIP

To prepare gelatine, place the crystals in a small bowl. Add enough water to dissolve (for one tablespoon of gelatin you will need no more than three tablespoons of water). Leave to stand at room temperature for a couple of minutes. Place the bowl on top of a warm oven or over hot water and stir until the gelatine is completely dissolved. Do not try any short cuts. You will end up with lumpy, crystallised gelatine.

END-OF-THE-MONTH COOKING

CHEESE AND CUMIN SCONES / MEXICAN OMELETTE / BREAD AND BUTTER PUDDING / TOMATO AND CHEESE TART

CHEESE AND CUMIN SCONES

Makes 12

INGREDIENTS

250 gms plain flour (maida)
1 tsp salt
2 tsps baking powder
50 gms cold butter, cut into small cubes
½ cup milk
½ cup water
150 gms cheddar cheese, grated
½ tsp Kashmiri chilli powder
1 tsp cumin, roasted on a tawa and slightly crushed

METHOD

Sift together the flour, salt and baking powder. Mix the butter into the flour until it resembles fine breadcrumbs. Blend in the cheese and chilli powder. Gradually add the milk and water, mixing it with a round-bladed knife or by hand until the dough is soft and manageable. Reserve a little milk for brushing the scones.

Turn the dough onto a lightly floured surface, divide into equal portions and knead each one lightly with the finger tips. Shape each portion into a round or with a shaped cutter, ¾ inch thick and about 2 inches in diameter. Arrange them on a greased baking tray; prick the top with a fork and sprinkle with the cumin. Press down lightly. Brush with milk or egg wash.

Bake the scones in the center of a preheated oven at 200°C for 12-15 minutes. Cool slightly before serving. Serve as is or cut and spread with butter or cheese spread and a slice of tomato.

KITCHEN ESSENTIALS

Oven
Baking tray
Mixing bowl
Serving plate

TIP

Scones can be kept in an airtight container for upto a week. For that `freshly baked` flavour, just pop them in the oven for two minutes before serving.

To make even lighter scones, add the equivalent amount of soda bicarbonate and cream of tartar (available at chemists and supermarkets) instead of baking powder.

MEXICAN OMELETTE

Serves 3-4

INGREDIENTS

6 eggs
6 tbsps butter
1 small onion, thinly sliced
1 green chilli, cut into stripes
½ kg tomatoes, skinned, seeded and chopped
2 tbsps tomato purée
100 gms cheddar cheese, grated
salt and pepper

METHOD

Melt half the butter in a large frying pan.
Add onion and cook over medium heat until soft, not brown. Stir in chilli, tomatoes and tomato purée. Simmer for 10 minutes. Season with salt and pepper.
Meanwhile whisk the eggs in a bowl. Add butter to a frying pan and heat. Pour in the eggs. Cook on a slow fire. Keep lifting the edges of the cooked mixture.
When the egg is still runny, add the tomato mixture on half of the surface. Top with cheese. Flip over the other half of the omelette. Cover with a lid and cook for two minutes. Slide out of the pan.

KITCHEN ESSENTIALS

Frying pan with lid
Serving plate

TIP

For a lighter omelette, add two tablespoons of water to the egg mixture while whisking.

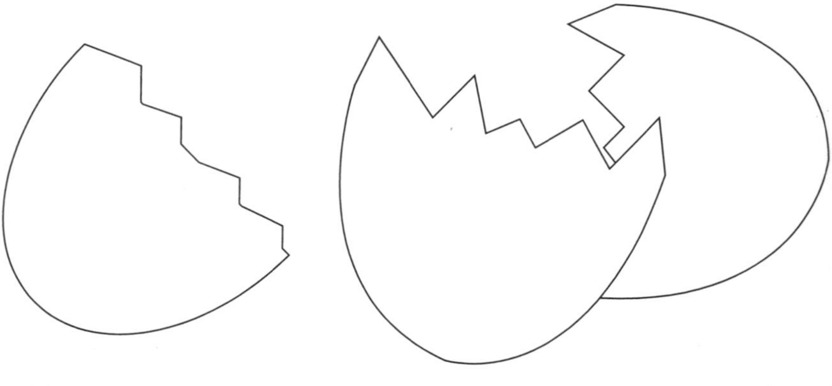

BREAD AND BUTTER PUDDING

Serves 4

INGREDIENTS

¼ cup butter
8 slices white bread
50 gms Yellow raisins (kismis)
2 large eggs
6 tbsps castor sugar
few drops vanilla essence
500 ml milk

METHOD

Butter a large oven-proof dish. Butter the slices of bread and cut them into quarters. Arrange the slices in the dish in alternate layers with the raisins. Do not overlap the slices of bread; cut them to fit the dish if necessary, finish with a layer of bread – butter side up. Beat the eggs with all but a tablespoon of sugar and vanilla essence. Bring the milk almost to the boil, then pour onto the beaten eggs. Pour mixture over the bread. Sprinkle the remaining sugar on top. Leave to stand for 15 minutes, to allow the bread to absorb the custard. Bake in a preheated oven for 30 minutes, until the pudding is set and lightly browned on top.

KITCHEN ESSENTIALS

Oven
Baking dish
Whisk
Mixing bowl
Serving bowls

TIP

Grated lime rind added to the custard, or cinnamon sprinkled on top before baking will vary the flavour.

TOMATO AND CHEESE TART
Serves 4

INGREDIENTS
1 large pizza base
1 egg yolk, beaten
1 tsp Karen Anand's whole-grain mustard
60 gms cheddar cheese, shaved with a vegetable peeler
6 small tomatoes
½ tsp dried thyme
salt and pepper
2 tbsps olive oil

METHOD
Preheat the oven to 180°C. Place the pizza base on a baking sheet and glaze a 1 inch band around the edge with the egg yolk.
Smear the centre with the mustard. Place a wafer-thin layer of cheddar on top of the mustard. Thinly slice the tomatoes and overlap on top of the cheese. Sprinkle over a little thyme, salt, olive oil and pepper.
Transfer to the oven and bake for 20 minutes, or until golden brown on top and the bottom crisp.

KITCHEN ESSENTIALS
OTG
Baking tray
Plate for serving

TIP
This is an easy pizza substitute.

Food

FOR ... THE DESI GUY

6

KEBAB MEIN HADDI

CHICKEN KAINCHI KEBAB / FISH TIKKA / SHIKAMPUR KEBABS

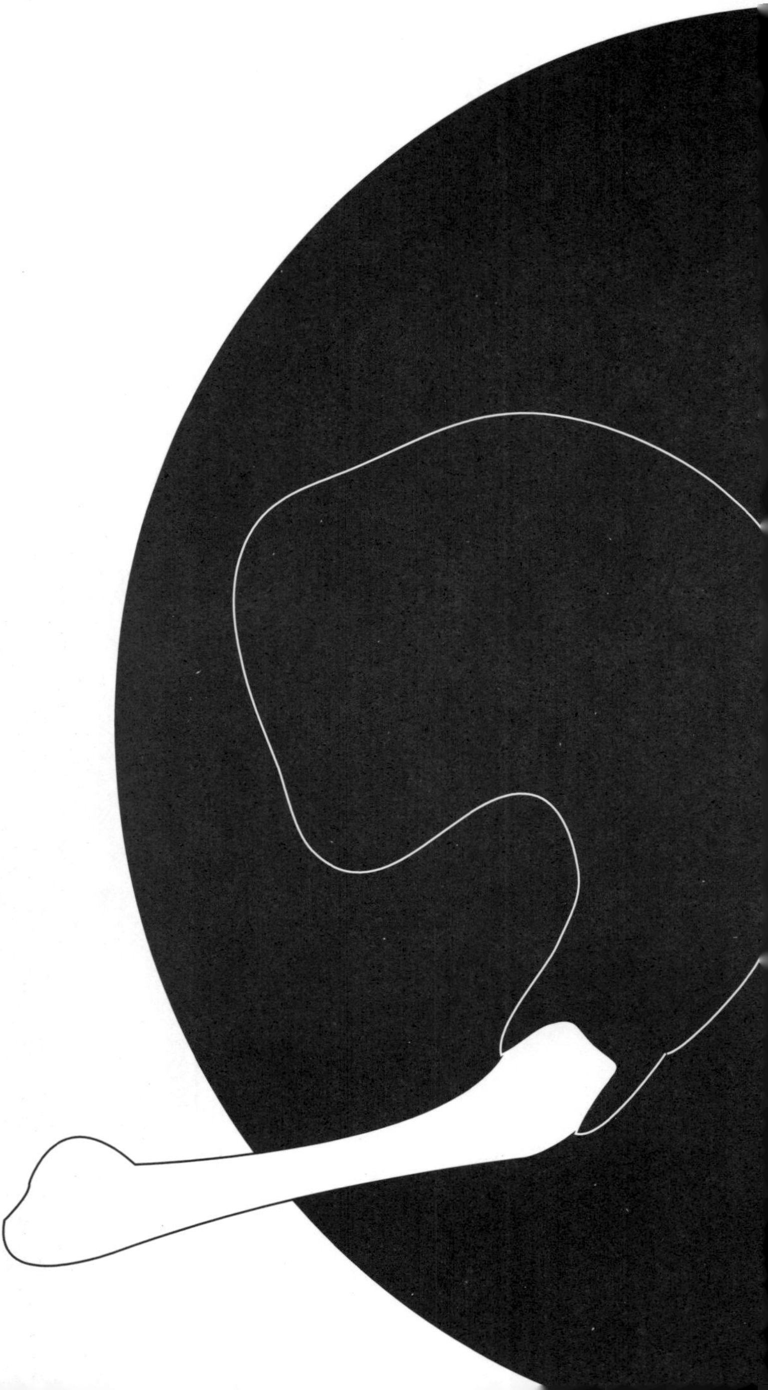

The problem with great chefs is that deep down they are people who love cooking and eating simple food. Somewhere along the way, something happens. They are forced to constantly "create" new dishes, come up with new twists to old themes and for want of a better expression, re-invent the wheel. Such is the case of the old charmer, the inimitable maestro of masala, whose forefathers cooked for the Nawabs of Avadh, Imtiaz Quereshi. What can I say, the man had me speechless (and for those who know me well, that's saying something!) with his deft hand, his amazing accuracy and the way he cleverly manoeuvred the conversation to something else, everytime I asked him for his recipe for Garam Masala (undoubtedly one of his real secret weapons). At the age of 71, I thought you were supposed to either put yourself out to graze somewhere or turn religious or both. The man is still a magician. It is astonishing that at his age and with the kind of reputation he has, he can still be flexible enough to find and create new recipes.

His personal favourites, he says, are dishes cooked by the women of his family, simple everday dals and kormas. Was he still capable of cooking a simple recipe though, the kind you whip up in a couple of minutes, which do not need a thousand complicated ingredients which require you to trek to several areas of town? Within a second, he asked for some breast of chicken and a pair of scissors. "I am going to show you Kainchi kebab. This was invented when there was left over raw Chicken or Mutton, intended for Pasanda, in the house." We worked with chicken and mutton, although he insisted that "Delhi has the best mutton in the country". He sprinkled a bit of this and that, asked me to mix the lot and watched carefully out of the corner of his eye, as if to test my skills. Within a minute, the kebabs were dusted with besan, deep fried and walloped by all of us. It was perfection. Please try it. The true test of a great chef is impromptu cooking. Imtiaz Quereshi is certainly one of our all-time greats.

CHICKEN KAINCHI KEBAB

Serves 2-3

INGREDIENTS

250 gms boneless chicken, cut into finger-sized pieces
chickpea flour (besan)
sunflower oil for frying

For the marinade

1 tsp salt
1 tbsp green chillies, finely chopped
1 tsp Great Garam Masala
1 tsp black pepper
1 tbsp ginger garlic paste
½ tsp red chilli powder
juice of 1 lime

Great garam masala

cardamom
cumin
bay Leaf
coriander whole
cloves
cinnamon
nutmeg
mace
aniseed
star anise

METHOD

Mix the chicken with all the ingredients, one at a time. Marinate for 5 minutes. Dust with chickpea flour and deep-fry in hot oil. When golden, remove, drain and eat as is. No chutney is actually required.

KITCHEN ESSENTIALS

Mixing bowl
Frying pan
Plate to serve

TIP

Use a deep-fat fryer and heat oil to 160°C. Your chicken will be perfectly cooked in just 5 minutes. Drain on absorbent paper. This makes an excellent cocktail snack and a healthy meal for children when they come home from school. It can also be made with mutton with the addition of a little unripe papaya juice for tenderising.

FISH TIKKA

Serves 3-4

INGREDIENTS

For the first marination

600 gms fresh fish such as rawas or bekti, cut into 1½ inch boneless cubes
2 tsps ginger paste
3 tsps garlic paste
salt to taste
3 tsp lemon juice

For the second marination

½ cup yoghurt
½ cup processed cheese, grated
4 tbsps cream
1 egg
1 tbsp chickpea flour
a pinch each of cumin powder, green cardamom powder, black pepper powder, cinnamon powder, clove powder
½ tsp caraway seeds (ajwain)
a pinch of turmeric powder
1 tbsp fresh dill (suva), chopped
butter for basting

METHOD

Mix all the ingredients in the first marination. Rub the fish cubes with this marinade and keep for 10 minutes. Drain off all juices. For the second marination, whisk the yoghurt and cheese in a bowl, add the remaining ingredients. Whisk and rub the fish with this marinade. Keep for 30 minutes. Place the fish on a baking tray or foil paper and grill in a preheated oven at 220°C for 5 minutes. Baste with butter, turn over for 3-4 minutes. Serve with a crisp salad or cachumber.

KITCHEN ESSENTIALS

Mixing bowls
Oven/grill
Baking tray
Platter to serve

TIP

Use chunky white fish. Pomfret is a bit of a waste. Oily fish such as Mackerel or Sardines are not suitable. Imported Norwegian Salmon is outstanding.

SHIKAMPUR KEBABS

Approximately 10-12 Kebabs

INGREDIENTS

Group 1

½ kg boneless mutton
2 onions, sliced
¼ tsp ginger and ¼ tsp garlic, ground together into a paste
1 tsp red chilli powder
½ tsp turmeric powder
handful fresh coriander, chopped finely
salt to taste
2 tbsps channa dal

Goup 2

masalas to be finely ground
2 tsps chironji (charoli)
1 tbsp white poppy seed (khuskhus)
2 tbsps ground almonds or cashew nuts
5 green cardamoms, skin removed
5 cloves
1 egg white, beaten
chutney for stuffing

Chutney

100 gms cream cheese
½ onion
2 green chillies, finely chopped
2 tbsps coriander

Mix all the above ingredients together in a bowl. This chutney should be of a very thick consistency.

METHOD

Mix together all the items of Group 1 in a pan, cover and cook on a medium heat for 25 minutes, or pressure cook for 10 minutes. Remove the lid and stir occasionally until all the water dries up. Continue to stir until the meat turns a little brown in colour.

Remove from the fire and add to the ground masalas of Group 2. Grind this mixture to a fine paste. (This can be prepared in advance and set aside or in the fridge till required). Add the beaten egg white to the meat mixture. Take a little of the mixture in the palm of the hand, (slightly smaller than the size of a ping pong ball). Flatten the mixture and put a little chutney (approx. one teaspoon) into the centre of the meat mixture. Cover the stuffing with the meat on all sides, form into a round shape and flatten. Shallow-fry on both sides until dark brown. Drain oil and serve hot.

KITCHEN ESSENTIALS

Mixer grinder
Mixing bowls
Frying pan
Plate to serve

TIP

It helps to grease the hand with a little oil first to be able to make the kebabs successfully.

This recipe was given to me many years ago by Pasha (Mumtaz) Khan, a fabulous Hyderabadi cook who has managed to keep these precious traditions and recipes alive.

QUICK CURRIES

JARDALOO MURG / PRAWN BALCHAO / GOAN FISH CURRY / CHICKEN RAZALLA / THAI GREEN CURRY WITH VEGETABLES

JARDALOO MURG

Serves 4

INGREDIENTS

1 kg whole chicken (pre-cut)
½ cup oil
5 onions, thinly sliced
2 sticks cinnamon
2 cardamoms
10 cloves
2 bay leaves
1 tbsp ginger paste
1 tbsp garlic paste
2 tsps roasted chilli powder
1 tsp roasted cumin (jeera) powdered
salt to taste
3-4 tbsps Worcestershire sauce
200 gms dried apricots soaked in hot water
100 gms sali (potato straws)
hardboiled eggs (optional)

METHOD

Heat oil and fry onions until just starting to colour. Add cinnamon, cardamom, cloves and bay leaves and continue to cook until onions are well browned. Add a splash of hot water and scrape up all the browned bits in the pan.

Add the ginger, garlic, chilli and jeera. Fry for one minute and add the chicken. Brown well and then add hot water. Cover and cook on a slow fire until the chicken is almost done. Add salt and continue to cook until chicken is tender.

Add the Worcestershire sauce and heat through. Add apricots and the water in which the apricots were soaked. Stir and serve hot with sali and hard-boiled eggs. Best with Basmati rice or saffron pullau.

KITCHEN ESSENTIALS

Handi
Serving bowl

TIP

This is a recipe from my friend Parvana Boga Noorani shared whilst shooting the Good Food Guide on Star Plus many moons ago.

PRAWN BALCHAO
Serves 4-6

INGREDIENTS
500 gms peeled, deveined fresh prawns
2 tbsps dried prawns, roasted and powdered
5 large onions, chopped fine
1 cup vinegar
1 cup ketchup
2 ½ cups vegetable oil
200 gms sugar
a few curry leaves
salt to taste

For the paste
20 Kashmiri chillies
2 inch piece of ginger
20 garlic cloves
½ tsp turmeric powder (haldi)
2 tbsps mustard seeds
2 tbsps cumin seeds
2 tsps black pepper corns

METHOD
Pat dry the cleaned prawns and soak for half an hour in the vinegar. Heat oil in a pan on medium heat. Sauté the onions, curry leaves, and spice paste until well cooked. Add the rest of the ingredients and the fresh prawns with the vinegar.
Lower flame and stirring continuously cook, for a further 5 to 7 minutes till the oil comes to the surface. Add salt to taste. Serve with hot bread or as a pickle.

KITCHEN ESSENTIALS
Mixer grinder
Bowl to soak
Frying pan
Serving bowl

TIP
Don't be tempted to use frozen prawns for this recipe. They will turn rock hard after cooking. If you are going to eat the dish immediately then you can even lightly fry the prawns separately and add at the last minute. Soaking in vinegar is a method used in Goa to preserve the prawns in this pickle.

GOAN FISH CURRY
Serves 4-6

INGREDIENTS
500 gms fish, slices or fillets
4-5 pieces kokum
2 ½ cups thick coconut milk
1 cup thin coconut milk (if using re-constituted or tetra pak, dilute with water)
salt to taste

Masala paste
10 Kashmiri chillies
1 tsp black peppercorns
1 tsp whole cumin
¼ tsp turmeric
10 cloves garlic
1" piece ginger
1 tbsp sesame seeds
½ tsp whole coriander

METHOD
Grind masala paste with a little water until very fine. Put in a handi along with the thin coconut milk and cook the paste on a low flame. This will take about 7-10 minutes.
Add the thick coconut milk a little at a time. Throw in the kokum and simmer. Add fish. Heat through once. Add salt to taste. Take care not to boil. The oil should not come to the surface. Serve with plain boiled rice, white or red Goan rice.

KITCHEN ESSENTIALS
Mixer grinder
Frying pan
Serving bowl

TIP
This is my family's traditional fish curry. You can substitute prawns for fish. Pieces of raw mango (without the skin) are also delicious instead of kokum as a souring agent.

CHICKEN RAZALLA
Serves 4-6

INGREDIENTS
1 kg whole chicken (pre-cut)
5 tbsps sunflower oil or ghee
8 cloves
1 tsp pepper
2 inch piece cinnamon
2 green cardamoms
2 black cardamoms
2 tbsps garlic paste
2 tbsps ginger paste
2 onions, made into a paste
1 kg yoghurt
1 kg chopped coriander leaves
10 green chillies (whole)
salt to taste

METHOD
Heat the oil in a thick-bottomed vessel. Add whole spices. Sauté garlic paste, ginger and onion paste untill the oil separates. Add a little water to avoid burning. Add chicken pieces and sear (brown) well.
Pour in the yoghurt and cook untill the chicken is tender. Add chopped coriander leaves, green chillies and salt to taste. Mix well until all the coriander is incorporated into the gravy.

KITCHEN ESSENTIALS
Handi
Serving bowl

TIP
We have made yoghurt for this receipe. For some reason, commercially available branded dahi tends to curdle when heated. If this happens, rescue it by whisking in a little cream.

THAI GREEN CURRY WITH VEGETABLES

Serves 4

INGREDIENTS

300 gms vegetables, diced
2 tbsps vegetable oil
20 gms Thai green curry paste
1 tbsp fish sauce
2 cups coconut milk
5 basil leaves
4 red chillies, sliced
3 stalks lemon grass
2 kaffir lime leaves
1 tsp sugar

METHOD

Fry the Thai green curry paste in 2 tablespoons of oil. As the oil separates, add the fish sauce, coconut milk, basil leaves and the vegetables. Cook till done.

Add the lemon grass and kaffir lime leaves. Taste and season with a little sugar. Garnish with red chillies and serve with plain steamed rice.

KITCHEN ESSENTIALS

Handi
Serving bowl

TIP

Thai Green Curry Paste is easily available in packets and bottles.

FOREWORD

Clearly men are from Mars and women most definitely are from Venus. Go and sit in a restaurant at lunch time and you'll find most of the female population munching on salads or nibbling on a snack. Guys however, left to their own devices, will order something meaty, cheesy or eggy. Basically, something oversized and chunky on a plate. So this chapter guys, is totally dedicated to you! Recipes to make your mouth water and to satisfy your souls. Comfort food at its best.

Food

THAT . . . GUYS LOVE

7

SAY CHEESE

ROASTED CHILLI & CORIANDER DIP / QUESADILLAS (HOT MEXICAN TORTILLAS WITH MELTED CHEESE & SALSA) / CHEESY CHICKEN KIEV / CHEESE FONDUE

All of a sudden, cheese and wine is all the rage. The French refer to cheese as part of their "Holy Trilogy"- bread, cheese and wine. They produce hundreds of varieties, from unpasteurised milk, the old fashioned way, pressed and cooked. And there is something for every palate – strong smelling or gently perfumed, soft and runny or firm and full of holes, blue veined or white as snow. Cheese is definitely an acquired taste. It smells like old socks to some but is like nectar to others. Some are used for cooking in dishes such as fondue, raclette, soufflés, omelettes, gratins (baked dishes), in sauces and in salads. In Europe, they are served as table cheeses to savour as a snack or more commonly, after a meal. Cheeses today are being used on pizzas, tacos, toast, served on a cheese board at society dinners or just munched as a delectable snack. Chefs are using cheese to stuff dosas and parathas, to melt in pancakes and to add life to dips. How do you know what they all taste like and the one best suited to your needs? Where do you get them? What can you expect to pay? And how, with the smell the way it is, can you distinguish the fresh from the rancid? Here are some guidelines to what you can expect.

BLUE

You either love or hate these natural cheeses, which have been injected with a penicillin fungus to produce blue veins. The most notorious of all cheeses, it is only appreciated by real connoisseurs and amateurs should tread carefully. They have an overbearing aroma and a very sharp taste.

The three Great Blues are Roquefort, made from sheep's milk and ripened in limestone caves in France; Gorgonzola, a creamy blue which comes from the village of the same name in Italy, and English Stilton. Danish Blue has been the most accessible of the "Blue Brigade" in India but isn't a patch on the other big "blues" in terms of taste, pungency and flavour.

Avoid blue cheese which has any signs of `greyness' or looks dry. Store well wrapped in the fridge away from any delicate foods. If stored properly it should last 2 to 3 weeks in the fridge. Ideal as an after dinner cheese or in a salad dressing.

There is some difference of opinion about which wines go with Roquefort. Personally, I prefer a well structured Bordeaux like Saint Emilion but modernists go for a fruity white, like Muscat de Rivesaltes or the more delicate Muscat de Beaumes de Venise.

BRIE & CAMEMBERT

Soft, creamy cheeses, which have an edible, white surface mould. Brie, like it's cousin or rather it's son Camembert (since Brie is older) is always in the shape of a disc and is nearly always mild, buttery and flavourful. Avoid cheeses that smell like ammonia. This is not a feature of the cheese. It has just overripened and should be thrown away. Always look for a surface, which may range from snowy white in younger cheeses to creamy with a little coloration around the edge. Danish Brie in tins is widely available in cities in India but quite inferior to the real French Brie which you buy as a 14 inch diameter wheel or wedges of that disc. Keep at room temperature for an hour and try to attack before it goes runny. Brie is a table cheese best with walnuts and fresh fruit unless fancy chefs decide to put it into a soufflé. Camembert and Brie can be eaten with light red wines such as Cotes du Rhone or Brouilly. In Normandy, where Camembert is made, it is often accompanied by local cider.

GRUYÈRE AND EMMENTAL

Gruyère comes from the mountainous areas of France and Switzerland. Like its cousin Emmental, it has a sweet, dry flavour with a nutty after-taste. It is harder and has fewer holes than Emmental. Keeps for several weeks in the fridge, if wrapped properly. Is ideal for after dinner. Gruyère with dried fruit and nuts is used in a traditional fondue along with Emmental or in any cheese sauce. These cheeses are very flexible and go with both crisp white wines as well as reds.

GOAT CHEESE

These are white, sometimes dusted with ash, which is good for digestion, made in the form of pyramids or logs or tiny rounds known as "crottin", which literally means "little lumps of shit", presumably referring to the shape and size, not the smell or taste! Goat cheeses start off their lives white and mild and become hard as they get older. They are basically table cheeses but are also melted on toast and used in salads. They have a peculiar flavour which you either love or hate.

Goat cheeses are never accompanied by red wines. They are best eaten with whites like Sancerre which comes from an area which produces the famous "Crottin de Chavignol". A light Rosé is also fine.

EDAM

This round, cannonball shaped Dutch cheese with a coating of red wax, is a family favourite world-wide. It is a natural, semi-firm cheese, which has a distinctive flavour, which is neither bland nor sharp. This is an ideal table and sandwich cheese and not suitable for cooking as it does not melt too well because of its relatively low fat content. Very good on a cheeseboard with apples. It also keeps very well in the fridge if you wrap the exposed area after cutting with cling film. Avoid cheese which has cracks or splits.

MOZZARELLA

A soft, white, bland tasting cheese which is used almost always for pizzas because of its stretchability and quick melting properties. Being fresh, it does not last very long and tends to sour. Look for shiny smooth, moist, creamy white cheese with an elastic texture. If the Mozzarella is vacuum packed, it is likely to last longer. Today, India produces some excellent Mozzarella.

GOUDA

A firm, sliceable cheese with a buttery taste, which deepens as it matures. It has a yellow wax rind and is creamier than Edam. Keeps for several weeks in the fridge. Is both a great table and cooking cheese. Smoked Gouda is made by natural smoking techniques or by using an artificial essence. Gouda produced in India is exceptionally good.

PROCESSED CHEESES

These are cheeses, which have a mild flavour and are constant and uniform in taste and texture. They are actually made by stopping the ripening action by heat. As a result these cheeses are less prone to spoilage. They are good for both sandwiches and snacks as well as for cooking and are relatively inexpensive compared with natural cheeses. The ones produced in India are very good. I recommend Britannia for cooking since it melts easily.

CHEDDAR

A natural, English-style hard cheese, which can range from mild and mellow to rich and nutty. Lasts for ages in the fridge. Perfect for baked dishes. Avoid cheese with cracks or drying edges and a strong, sour smell. The ones produced in India are sold young. Perfect if you are a cheese lover and prefer a natural taste.

CREAM CHEESES

These range from the health conscious cottage cheese to the creamier paneer and Philadelphia cream cheese. These are usually used for creamy cheese cakes or piled onto smoked salmon, celery or more commonly, used as a base for dips.

PARMESAN

This Queen of Italian cheeses is the Italian 'cure all' for everybody from the age of six to sixty! It is hard and crumbly, with a grainy texture and has a sharp aroma and piquant flavour. It is probably the world's favourite "gourmet" grating cheese. Parmesan comes from Parma in northern Italy and is aged for at least two to three years. It is always in the form of a large, deep wheel and lasts forever thanks to its low moisture content and hard texture. Parmesan is best bought from the wheel itself. Parmigiano Reggiano is the best variety money can buy. You can also buy it already grated in packets, which is a fair substitute for sprinkling on pasta but there is nothing quite like the original as both a table cheese with figs, peaches and grapes, or grated in soups, pastas and rice dishes.

CHEESY QUESTIONS

How Fattening is Cheese?

Cream cheese has a fat content of approximately 28 per cent. Processed cheese has approximately 26-27 per cent, which includes cheese spreads too. Natural Cheddar has 36 per cent. To give you a comparison; butter is 80 per cent fat and most oils, 100 per cent fat !!!!!

Health Factors

Cheese is an ideal concentrated protein food. When eaten at the end of a meal it assists in the prevention of dental cavities because of its alkaline content. Despite a wide variety of flavours and textures, the nutritional value of hard cheeses is very similar. They provide an excellent source of calcium and phosphorous, a moderate source of protein and vitamin A. They are high in saturated fat with moderate amounts of cholesterol.

How to Store

Cheese is usually wrapped in greaseproof paper and kept on a window sill or in the cold part of the house in Europe. However in India, with our humidity and heat, I find it better to wrap cheese in foil or cling film and keep it in the warmest part of the refrigerator (cheese compartment) or in the vegetable tray. Try not to freeze cheese. Freezing will affect the taste, texture and meltability. Cheese has to breathe to maintain life and vigour. Don't be afraid of a bit of mould. This is a sign that the cheese is 'natural' with no preservatives. Just cut or scrape it off and use the rest.

ROASTED CHILLI AND CORIANDER DIP

Serves 4-6

INGREDIENTS

4 green chillies
1 large tomato, chopped
250 gms cream cheese
2 spring onions, finely chopped
2 tbsps chopped fresh coriander
2 tbsps fresh lime juice

METHOD

Roast the chillies under a grill or over a flame until the skins are blackened on all sides. Wearing rubber gloves to protect your fingers, scrape the charred skins off the chillies. Cut off the stalks and remove seeds. Chop finely.

Put the chillies, tomato and remaining ingredients in a bowl, then blend with a fork until well blended. Serve at room temperature with vegetable sticks (cucumber, carrot, radish, red and green capsicum), wafers or tortilla chips. Always store in the refrigerator.

KITCHEN ESSENTIALS

OTG
Mixing bowl
Serving bowl and plate or chip 'n' dip dish

TIP

Keep the cream cheese out of the fridge for at least half an hour to be able to soften it. Alternatively put it straight from the fridge into a blender with a tablespoon or two of warm water.

QUESADILLAS

(HOT MEXICAN TORTILLAS WITH MELTED CHEESE AND SALSA)
Serves 4

INGREDIENTS

8 rotis made from wheat flour (atta)
2 tbsps oil
2 cups grated processed cheese
1 jar Karen Anand's spicy Mexican salsa

METHOD

Heat a tawa or a non-stick pan over medium heat. Add half a tablespoon of oil. When hot, place one roti on the pan: sprinkle with one-fourth cup of grated cheese, one-fourth cup of spicy mexican salsa and top with another one-fourth cup of grated cheese. Top with a second roti and press slightly. Cook until the cheese has melted and the bottom roti is golden brown. Using a spatula, flip; cook until golden on both sides, and until the cheese melts inside. Cut into wedges. Repeat with remaining ingredients. Serve hot as a snack.

KITCHEN ESSENTIALS

Tawa
Plate to serve

TIP

For a non-veg version, add cooked chicken mince or diced roast chicken before adding the final layer of cheese.

CHEESY CHICKEN KIEV

Serves 2

INGREDIENTS

2 large chicken boneless breast fillets
200 gms cheese spread
grated rind and juice of a small lime
1 tsp mustard powder
2 tbsps fresh chopped dill or parsley
pinch of ground nutmeg
salt and black pepper
1 large egg
1 cup fresh white breadcrumbs
oil for deep-frying

METHOD

Cream the cheese spread in a bowl with the lime rind, mustard, dill or parsley and a pinch of nutmeg. Season to taste with salt, freshly ground pepper and a little lime juice. Leave in the freezer until it has set almost hard.

Lay the breast fillets between sheets of greaseproof paper and beat them flat. Season with salt and pepper. Cut the cheese, spread into four finger-length pieces and place one in the center of each chicken fillet. Fold the edges over neatly and roll the fillet up tightly. Secure with fine string, if necessary.

Beat the egg lightly and brush over the chicken rolls before coating them evenly with breadcrumbs; press them in thoroughly. The chicken rolls may be coated a second time for a crisper finish, patting the egg on with a brush so as not to disturb the first coating. Roll again in crumbs.

Leave the rolls in the fridge until the coating has set for about an hour. Heat the oil in a deep fryer or kadhai. Fry the chicken rolls in two batches, until golden brown for around six minutes. Drain the rolls on crumpled absorbent paper. Arrange the chicken rolls on a warmed serving dish.

Boiled potatoes tossed in butter and leeks make good side dishes with the chicken or serve hot simply as a hearty snack.

KITCHEN ESSENTIALS

Mixing bowls
Deep fat fryer or kadhai
Serving plate

CHEESE FONDUE

Serves 4

INGREDIENTS

1 clove garlic
3 cups cheddar cheese, grated
1½ cups white wine (Chantilli Chardonnay or Riviera are perfect)
1 tsp lime juice
2 tsps cornflour
3 tbsps vodka (since kirsch is not available in India)
½ tsp black pepper
1 tsp ground nutmeg
white bread cubes (about 1 cup per person)

METHOD

Rub the inside of a heat resistant, ceramic pot or non-stick sauce pan with the garlic clove. Bring the wine and lime juice to a boil, stirring constantly. Add cheese. Combine the cornflour and kirsch or vodka and add them to the cheese, then season with pepper and nutmeg.

Cook the cheese until it is smooth and creamy, and then place the pan over an alcohol lamp at the table. Let the fondue continue to bubble during the meal and stir it from time to time so that it stays creamy. Spear the bread cubes with fondue forks and dip into the cheese.

KITCHEN ESSENTIALS

Fondue pot
Fondue forks
Non-stick saucepan

TIP

If the fondue is too thin, add more grated cheese; if it is too thick, thin it with wine. In the original recipe, Swiss cheeses like Emmental and Gruyère are used in varying proportions, depending on the region. But even the Swiss are now experimenting with different cheeses and replacing wine sometimes with cider.

EGGCITING EGGVENTURES

EGGS ON TOMATOES / STUFFED EGGS / CARAMEL CUSTARD / SOUFFLÉ WELSH RAREBIT

For years poultry has been used as a ceremonious centerpiece for the dining table. It is healthy, satisfying and appeals to the most finicky palates. It is perhaps appropriate, in the wake of bird flu, to bring up the hygiene element as well. India is considered to have the most organized and hygienic poultry sector in the world. This applies to the processing of frozen and pre-cut chicken as well. Phew! What a relief.

You may not realise that chicken is actually descended from the wild red jungle fowl of India. It was then taken to China, the Pacific Islands, then finally to the countries of the Mediterranean, where eggs were first eaten rather than the "scrawny chicken". Europeans only started eating chicken as late as the thirteenth century.

Poultry and eggs contain a full compliment of the nine essential amino acid protein building blocks. These are required for the growth and development of children. One egg supplies more than an adult's daily requirement of Vitamin B12.

Chicken is an excellent source of protein, which is easily digested. An average 140 gms serving of chicken provides more than half a man's daily requirement and a considerable amount of iron.

The popularity of chicken and eggs mean that my ingenuity is constantly exercised by the need to invent new and exciting recipes for you to try. Chicken and eggs are a joy to work with. They are versatile and lend themselves to a wide range of cuisines.

EGGS ON TOMATOES

Serves 3-4

INGREDIENTS

6 eggs
1 kg tomatoes, blanched, peeled and chopped
5 onions, chopped
1 stick of cinnamon
2-3 cloves
2 tsps chilli powder
1 tbsp garlic paste
3 tbsps malt vinegar
½ cup fresh coriander chopped
salt to taste
1½ tsps sugar
1 tbsp Worcestershire sauce

METHOD

Put the tomatoes, onions, cinnamon, cloves, garlic paste and chilli paste into a handi and simmer until the sauce thickens. Depending on the tomatoes, this could take anywhere from 10 to 20 minutes. Add fresh coriander and salt and cook for a further 5-10 minutes until the tomatoes are reduced to a thick purée. Add the sugar, vinegar and Worcestershire sauce and salt to taste. Allow to cook for a couple more minutes to blend the flavours.

Remove the pan from the heat. Discard the cinnamon and cloves. Spread the mixture evenly in an ovenproof dish. Make six depressions in the mixture with the back of a spoon. Carefully break an egg into each depression. Cover with foil and bake in a medium oven until the eggs have just set. Serve immediately.

KITCHEN ESSENTIALS

Saucepan or handi
OTG
Oven-proof dish
Serving plate

TIP

This is a typical Parsi recipe, 'tamatar par enda' which satisfies the need for a "wholesome meal" even when there is no meat.

STUFFED EGGS

Serves 3-4

INGREDIENTS

6 hard-boiled eggs, halved lengthwise
½ container pepper or garlic cheese spread
1 small onion very finely chopped
1 small green capsicum, seeded and very finely chopped
125 gms cooked prawns, shelled de-veined and chopped
1 tsp lime juice
dash of Worcestershire sauce
salt and pepper
large pinch red chilli powder
shredded lettuce and sliced tomato to serve
1 tbsp finely chopped coriander, to garnish

METHOD

Using a teaspoon, scoop out the egg yolks into the food processor or blender; blend until smooth with the cheese spread or with a fork. Transfer to a medium bowl. Stir in the onion, green pepper, prawns, Worcestershire sauce, lime juice, salt, pepper and chilli powder.

Using a teaspoon, place generous amounts of the mixture into the egg whites.

Arrange on a bed of shredded lettuce and tomato slices. Sprinkle with coriander. Serve at room temperature.

KITCHEN ESSENTIALS

Food processor
Mixing bowl
Platter to serve

TIP

For a vegetarian version omit the prawns and add some chopped red bell pepper. For a healthier version replace the cooked prawns with 100 gms silken tofu which you can blend with the egg yolk and cheese spread.

CARAMEL CUSTARD
Serves 4

INGREDIENTS
2 eggs
2 egg yolks
3 tbsps castor sugar
350 ml milk

Caramel
1 cup castor sugar
½ cup water

METHOD
To make the caramel, dissolve sugar in water in a small sauce pan over moderate heat. Boil syrup steadily until a deep-golden caramel. Remove pan from heat and allow any bubbles to subside. Pour caramel into a glass bowl or jelly mould. Turn bowl carefully to coat sides evenly. Lightly whisk eggs, egg yolks and sugar together, then pour on milk. Whisk, then strain into the caramel lined dish. Place bowl in a baking dish and pour hot water into the dish to come just over half way up the sides of the bowl. Bake at 160 °C for 45 minutes until just set. Remove custard immediately from the baking dish and refrigerate overnight. To serve, place a deep plate over the custard and carefully turn it over. The custard should be surrounded by dark liquid caramel.

KITCHEN ESSENTIALS
Oven/Grill
Saucepan
Glass bowl
Oven proof dish
Bowl to serve

TIP
For a different flavour, infuse orange zest or Karen Anand's chunky orange marmalade in the hot milk for an hour before making the custard. Decorate with slices of fresh orange.

SOUFFLÉ WELSH RAREBIT

Serves 2

INGREDIENTS

4 slices whole meal bread
3 tbsps butter
2 tbsps plain flour
1½ cups milk
1 tsp Karen Anand's wholegrain mustard
1 tsp Worcestershire sauce
150 gms grated cheddar cheese
2 eggs, separated

METHOD

Melt the butter in a saucepan, stir in the flour and cook for one minute. Gradually stir in the milk and bring to the boil, stirring. Cook, stirring, over a low heat until thick. Remove from the heat and beat in the mustard, Worcestershire sauce, grated cheese and egg yolks. Cool slightly. Whisk the egg whites until stiff. Fold into the cheese mixture.

Spoon the mixture on top of the bread slices and place in an oven on a medium heat for 5-10 minutes or until puffed and golden. Serve immediately.

KITCHEN ESSENTIALS

OTG
Mixing bowl
Saucepan
Serving plate

TIP

White sauce can be made well in advance. Heat when required and then add the eggs. For a bit of spice, add two chopped green chillies to the egg and cheese mixture.

BOY MEETS GRILL (BARBECUES)

CLASSIC PEPPER STEAK / HONEY MUSTARD CHICKEN / SWEET POTATO & CARDAMOM BUTTER / CORN WITH CHILLI OIL

The men I have come across with an interest in food, seem to be most comfortable kneading a loaf of bread or in front of the flames of a barbecue. The bakery number attracts the quiet, precise scientific type, whereas the barbecue is the perfect place for the amateur cook and the macho Indiana Jones type.

To test the skills of men folk I know, I decided to have a barbecue in my garden. The best thing about cooking outdoors is that you don't have to nag anybody about the mess! A barbecue party combines all the pleasure of eating campfire food with the convenience of being in your own garden or terrace or even balcony and near your own kitchen. It is casual, unfussy and generally tends to result in a lot of letting down of the hair. The equipment need not be elaborate or expensive. We made a barbecue from bricks and cement and plastered on the front into the cement some oyster shells, the contents of which we walloped one Sunday. The rest, as they say, is history. A cast iron grill, some coal and a few logs of wood later, we have a center-piece to be proud of.

Now to the meat of it – there was fish actually. The red snapper was bathed in Thai red curry paste and Kaffir lime leaves and the sardines were sprinkled with coarse black pepper, oregano and olive oil. Then the guys cooked the lot. They looked, turned, tossed and commented. Finally, we had seafood to die for with a huge tossed salad and a siesta on the lawn. However, for the first time cook, simple cuts of meat and vegetables are preferable.

A barbecue party combines all the pleasure of eating quality, rustic food with the convenience of being in your own garden, balcony or terrace, near your own kitchen. The equipment need not be elaborate or expensive, but the food needs to be well chosen, simple, easy to prepare and the best quality you can find. During the rains, this is the kind of food you long for – comforting, tasty and satisfying. It is also a great way of getting men to start cooking by "playing with fire".

SETTING THE BARBECUE

Place the barbecue fairly close to the kitchen so that it is easy to carry things backwards and forwards, and also near a power point in case you need extension leads for lighting or music. Unless you have absolute confidence in a fine forecast, try to site it close to some sort of shelter or patio to which you can retreat if it rains. Alternatively, try to borrow or hire a canvas or tarpaulin canopy. As a last resort, cook the food on the barbecue outside the house, in the garage for example, keep it warm in the oven and serve it indoors. Never light a barbecue in a confined space, if there is not sufficient ventilation. If you have to cook in the garage, keep the doors wide open.

Position the barbecue between the tables from which the food is to be served and those, which hold the uncooked food and the cooking equipment. Keep the drinks separate from the food – this makes it easier to serve and cuts down on the chance of accidents.

LIGHTING

For an evening barbecue, lighting may be needed. The lights from the house or a few spotlights may be enough to eat by. Candles or nightlights such as in jam jars can be dotted around the garden. These can also be used to warn of possible dangers such as water bodies. Also available are flares, which are simply stuck into the ground and will burn for several hours. It is essential to have good lighting around the barbecue itself, both for safety and so that the cook can see what he/she is doing.

Prepare everything possible in advance. Once the cooking begins the cook needs to be able to concentrate on looking after the barbecue.

There are things you should bear in mind when choosing which dish to take to a barbecue. As well as dishes that actually improve by not being consumed as soon as they're made, try to ensure that your chosen recipe is easy to eat with your fingers if neccessary. After all, you never know whether you'll be sprawled on the lawn or formally seated at a table so finger food or bite-size pieces are best. You should also consider how you're going to transport it. Never make anything that can collapse or melt on the way.

Barbecues always take a while to get hot, so it's wise to serve some nibbly food to keep everyone going, or which can double up as an accompaniment should everything not run on time. I suggest a couple of dips or relishes or salsas with plenty of chips, or some delicious bread.

Lastly, think about how to make your chosen dish look stunning, even if you are serving it in plastic containers. Choose bright, colourful salads that will look appetizing and sprinkle with a fresh herb garnish. A handful of coriander leaves and some lime wedges, for example, will make an oriental coleslaw look as good as it tastes. If you wish to disguise your salad plate, why not line it with leaves?

To the food itself. Your ingredients have to be top notch, the best quality you can find. You cannot mask bad cuts of meat or two-day-old vegetables with dubious gravies and sauces. This is dry food. If it is old or fatty or has seen the inside of a fridge for too long, it will taste like that. Everything must be absolutely fresh.

Lastly, what to drink. Fancy wines and cocktails to my mind do not go with hard core "barbies". The only thing you really need is good, chilled beer, preferably easy to hold, pint-sized bottles. Fosters is ideal, for several reasons. It is a quality beer made from only Melbourne standard water, so the taste is the same wherever you go. Because of the amber coloured bottles, it is also less prone to spoilage from the sun and heat. However, you must remember that the glasses you serve in must be completely grease free and clean, otherwise you'll have flat beer on your hands.With all these tips, your barbecue is bound to be a stomping success!

CLASSIC PEPPER STEAK

Serves 4-6

INGREDIENTS

1 kg fillet (undercut), cut into 1½ inch thick steaks (should give you 5 big steaks)
1 tbsp butter
1 tbsp olive oil
sea salt
4 tbsps brandy
4 tbsps cream

For the marinade

3 tbsps red wine vinegar or ½ cup red wine
3 cloves garlic, crushed
1 tsp sea salt
2 tbsps green Kerala peppercorn or 1 tbsp freshly ground black pepper
3 tbsps olive oil
1 tsp mixed herbs (dry)

METHOD

Marinate the steaks for at least one hour. Cook the steaks over high heat for two minutes, turning them once to seal the juices. Cook for 5 minutes for rare steaks, 8-10 minutes for medium-rare and 12 minutes for well-done steaks. Baste with olive oil and butter mixture. Sprinkle with sea salt. Lift the steaks on to a hot serving dish. Put the remaining marinade in a pan. Warm the brandy in a ladle. Pour over the juices. Set alight when hot.

Draw the pan off the heat and as soon as the flames have died down, strain the juices and return to the pan. Gradually stir in the cream. Keep warm. Season the sauce with salt and pepper and pour it over the steaks.

KITCHEN ESSENTIALS

Mixing bowl
Saucepan
Frying pan
Serving plate

TIP

To keep each steak intact, tie with a twine, which can be removed before serving. Can be cooked on a barbecue or in a frying pan.

HONEY MUSTARD CHICKEN

Serves 4

INGREDIENTS

8 chicken drumsticks
4 tbsps olive oil
3 tbsps Karen Anand's wholegrain mustard
2 tbsps honey
2 tbsps lime juice
1 tbsp Karen Anand's Szechwan sauce
salt

METHOD

Wipe the chicken drumsticks with kitchen paper. Cut two or three deep slashes in the flesh of each drumstick and then place them in a deep bowl. Mix together the wholegrain mustard, honey, Szechwan sauce or chilli paste, olive oil, salt and lime juice and mix with the chicken.

Leave to marinate in a cool place, turning occasionally, or overnight in the fridge. Place the drumsticks on the barbecue. When golden, turn over. (this should take approx 10-12 minutes). Serve at once.

KITCHEN ESSENTIALS

OTG
Mixing bowls
Serving plate

TIP

Can be easily done in an oven or even in a frying pan. In case of an oven, preheat to 250°C, place the chicken in the oven to brown for 5–7 minutes and reduce temperature to 180°C. In a frying pan, sear the chicken on high flame and reduce flame and cook chicken with the lid on.

SWEET POTATO AND CARDAMOM BUTTER

Serves 1

INGREDIENTS

1 sweet potato
¼ tsp cardamom powder
4 tbsps butter
1 tsp jaggery

METHOD

Boil the sweet potato without peeling it. Mix together 4 tablespoons of butter, one-fourth teaspoon of cardamom and one teaspoon of jaggery. Slit or cut the potato and put the butter mixture into the slits while the potato is still hot. Put it back on the barbecue to singe slightly. Serve at once.

KITCHEN ESSENTIALS

Handi
Mixing bowl
Serving plate

TIP

Cardamom powder is readily available. You can also make it by removing the skins of cardamom and powdering the seeds in a grinder or an old fashioned mortar and pestle.

CORN WITH CHILLI OIL
Serves 2

INGREDIENTS
2 American corn cobs
2 tbsps olive oil
1 tbsp butter
1 tsp chilli flakes
1 tsp lime juice
1 tsp salt
1 tsp sugar

METHOD
Break each cob into three pieces. Immerse in water till just covered. Add one teaspoon of salt and one teaspoon of sugar. Boil for five minutes and remove. Barbecue on a hot griddle until golden, taking care not to burn or blacken the corn.
Meanwhile heat the olive oil and butter in a small frying pan. Add chilli flakes and lime juice. Let the mixture sizzle for 30 seconds. Remove and pour over the corn.

KITCHEN ESSENTIALS
Large saucepan or handi
Small frying pan or BBQ
Plate to serve

TIP
Be careful not to boil corn for more than 5-7 minutes because it loses its taste. It can also be boiled in a microwave.

HINDI-CHINI BHAI-BHAI

HOT AND SOUR SOUP / HONEY CHILLI CHICKEN / CHOW MEIN / SPICY STIR-FRIED MUSHROOMS

HOT AND SOUR SOUP
Serves 4

INGREDIENTS
100 gms boneless chicken
6 pieces dried Chinese mushroom
250 gms fresh bean curd (tofu)
2 eggs
2 tsps sesame oil
1 litre chicken stock
2 tsps sugar
3 tbsps cider vinegar or Chinese vinegar
½ tsps white pepper
2 tbsps dark soya sauce
1 tbsp cornflour blended with 1 tbsp water
2 tbsps spring onions, finely chopped
2 tbsps fresh coriander, finely chopped

METHOD
Cut the chicken into thin shreds. Bring some water to a boil and blanch the chicken for two minutes. Drain the chicken and set it aside. Soak the mushrooms in warm water for 20 minutes, then drain them and squeeze out any excess liquid. Discard the stems and shred the caps finely.

Drain the bean curd and shred into thin strips. Beat the eggs and one teaspoon of sesame oil together in a small bowl. Bring the chicken stock to a simmer in a large pot. Add the prepared chicken, mushrooms, and bean curd together with the sugar, vinegar, white pepper and dark soya sauce. Simmer together for three minutes, and then thicken it with cornflour mixture. Simmer for two minutes with the heat as low as possible.

Next, pour the beaten egg mixture into the soup in a steady stream and pull the egg into strands with a fork. Stir in the spring onion, fresh coriander, and one teaspoon of sesame oil. Pour into soup bowls and serve at once.

KITCHEN ESSENTIALS
Large saucepan or handi
Bowls to soak
Mixing bowls
Soup bowls

TIP
The egg must be poured in when the soup is piping hot.

HONEY CHILLI CHICKEN

Serves 4

INGREDIENTS

750 gms boneless chicken breast (3 pcs)
1 tbsp chopped ginger
1 tbsp chopped garlic
4 tbsps oil
2 tbsps oyster sauce
4 tsps Karen Anand's Szechwan sauce
4 tbsps soya sauce
4 tbsps honey

METHOD

Fry the ginger and garlic in a little oil until golden brown. Add the rest of the ingredients except the chicken and cook through. Cool. Fry the chicken in the rest of the oil for three minutes on each side. Pour on the sauce and cook on a low heat with the lid on (braise) until the chicken is cooked through. You may need to add a little water if the sauce gets too thick.

KITCHEN ESSENTIALS

Frying pans
Serving plate

TIP

This is a wonderful recipe for a barbecue. Use the sauce as a marinade and pour onto the raw chicken. Toss the chicken onto a hot barbecue or grill and baste continuously with the leftover sauce.

CHOW MEIN
Serves 4

INGREDIENTS

200 gms egg noodles
100 gms boneless chicken breast
4 slices ham, finely chopped
3 tsps light soya sauce
2 tsps dry sherry or rice wine vinegar
4 tsps oil, preferably groundnut
1 tsp garlic, finely chopped
50 gms mange-tout, trimmed or French beans
½ tsp sugar
1 tbsp spring onions, finely chopped
1 tsp sesame oil
1 tsp cornflour

METHOD

If you are using dried noodles, soak them in warm water for 10 minutes. Slice the chicken breast into fine shreds, in two long. Combine the chicken shreds with the sherry or rice wine vinegar and corn flour in a small bowl. Mix well together and let the chicken marinate for about 10 minutes.

Heat two teaspoons of groundnut oil in a wok and stir-fry the chicken shreds for about two minutes and transfer to a plate. Clean the wok. Drain the noodles, shaking off as much excess water as possible.

Reheat the pan and add the remaining groundnut oil and garlic. Stir-fry for 10 seconds and add mange-tout or French beans and ham or salami. Stir-fry for about one minute and then add the noodles, soya sauce, sugar and spring onions. Continue to stir-fry for two minutes and then return the chicken to the noodle mixture. Continue to stir-fry for about three-four minutes or until the chicken is cooked.

Add the sesame oil and stir. Turn chow mein out onto a plate and serve.

KITCHEN ESSENTIALS

Wok or large frying pan
Bowl to soak
Platter to serve

Tip

If you are using quick instant noodles, just soak in water for 30 seconds and drain.

SPICY STIR-FRIED MUSHROOMS

Serves 4

INGREDIENTS

1 tbsp oil, preferably groundnut
1 tsp finely chopped fresh ginger
2 tsps finely chopped spring onions
1 tsp finely chopped garlic
450 gms button mushrooms, whole
1 tsp chilli sauce
2 tsps dry sherry or rice wine
2 tsps dark soy sauce
1 tbsp chicken stock or water
½ tsp sugar
¼ tsp salt
1 tsp sesame oil

METHOD

Heat a wok or large frying pan over a high heat until it is hot. Add the oil and then the ginger, spring onions and garlic. Stir-fry for about 20 seconds.
Then add the mushrooms and stir-fry them for about 30 seconds. Quickly add the rest of the ingredients except the sesame oil.
Continue to stir-fry for about five minutes or until the mushrooms are cooked through and have absorbed all the spices and seasonings. Just before serving, add the sesame oil and give the mixture a couple of quick stirs. Turn out onto a warm serving dish and serve at once.

KITCHEN ESSENTIALS

Wok or large frying pan
Serving dish

TIP

Do not be afraid of cooking on a very high flame. It is a very healthy way of fast frying using minimum oil.

Food

... TO END WITH

8

FOREWORD

Desserts are one thing. Chocolate is quite another. It is a mad, seductive, sinful addiction (chocoholism) which afflicts some of us most of the time. Most of the men I know have a sweet tooth. Some more than others. My husband for example, will rave about how he wants to eat something "light" for dinner " cut down on the oil" "go for grilling instead of frying" and so on, and then demolish a big bar of Lindt chocolate afterwards. Such are the idiosyncrasies of the male sweet tooth. It's not just my husband either. I can cite hundreds of similar examples of men who skip lunch or take the trouble to make an oil-free, fat-free meal and throw caution to the wind when it comes to ice cream, chocolate cake or cheesecake – Guys, let's not pretend any longer. Here are some of my tried and tested old favourites. Eat your heart out.

CHOCOHOLICS ANONYMOUS

ORANGE CHOCOLATE FONDUE / HOT CHOCOLATE SOUFFLÉ / SIMPLE CHOCOLATE CAKE

Everyone adores a proper pudding. By which I mean one that contains butter, sugar, flour, cream, fruit or preferably all five. If you have bought other bits rather than made them yourself, then you ought to show them willingly with a home-made pudding. Otherwise it might look as if you don't care.

If the meal has been light you could make a pie or tart, or even a cake. Try old-fashioned recipes that no one else bothers to make nowadays, like bread and butter pudding, rice pudding with gorgeous unusual jam, or how about a treacle tart with a bowl of cold, thick cream? Even if some guests may be clucking to themselves that you served bought rillettes or pate to start with, a home-made trifle, summer pudding or treacle sponge will soon shut them up.

Chocolates, the luxurious sort that cost a fortune, will make everyone's eyes light up. But I go one better. I offer a mixture, on a large dish, of everything from the most expensive handmade truffles to fingers of Kit Kat: from broken squares of top-notch dark almond chocolate to chocolate Brazils. I have even been known to slice up a cool Mars bar and wedge the pieces in amongst the rose creams and those strips of bitter chocolate-covered orange peel. Something for everyone. And don't forget to add a few After Eights, too.

You never fail with a good-quality store bought ice-cream. If you feel the need to trim it up, then serve it with poached fruits, with a vast, spilling bowl of scarlet berries or with crushed meringues and some raspberry purée made by pushing berries through a sieve and adding a little icing sugar or eau de vie de framboise.

\- **Nigel Slater**

In spite of all the chaos in the world, the festive season has begun, albeit in a much calmer mode. My advice to you is, forget all the noise and pollution and indulge in some sinful pleasures. If all else fails, chocolates will do too.

So, to celebrate, I asked a glamorous brunette to join me in the Cook-In this week at the Grand Maratha in Mumbai. Zeba Kohli, the name and the face behind Fantasie Chocolates has been running this family business for over ten years. In addition to making a range of mouthwatering chocolates, she also represents the famous Swiss chocolate makers, Lindt in India. Famous for their traditional Almond Rocks and Marzipan, Zeba has now stepped out of the traditional family mould to produce such scrumptious delights as truffles, which are basically good quality chocolate and cream, rolled together, including an outstanding Champagne truffle.

Gone are the days of the foil wrapped, hard as nails, chocolates. Zeba now plans to re-design her entire packaging and imaging to go with her new quality fare.
To accompany us, we had Matthew Cropp, then Executive Chef of the

Grand Maratha, and now Executive Chef of The Oberoi, Mumbai. What is wonderful about Matthew's style, is that he draws from his vast culinary experience in South East Asia to create dishes which make you say to yourself, "Why didn't I think of that ?" You won't find him serving just pineapple – no, he steeps it in a hint of sugar syrup and dunks in some cinnamon sticks for flavour. A simple tomato consommé is made fragrant and special with saffron and star anise. And so it goes with chocolates too. Rather than the traditional truffles, with a coating of dark chocolate, Matthew enrobes them with crushed pistachio or almonds, so they look like miniature mithai – a great idea for Diwali. To top it all, he places a stick of sugared vanilla bean into the chocolate box for that unmistakable aroma. Matthew sourced vanilla beans here in India, something I haven't able to do in 15 years!

ORANGE CHOCOLATE FONDUE

Serves 4

INGREDIENTS

¾ cup whipping cream
300 gms dark chocolate (preferably Lindt), chopped
1 box (125 gms) Lindt Orange Swiss Thins
1 tbsp butter
¼ cup Cointreau or Grand Marnier orange liqueur

Suggested Accompaniments

Strawberries, bananas, kiwi fruits, apples, pears, peaches, chikoos, sponge cake

METHOD

In a saucepan heat cream just to boiling. Remove from heat. Add both types of chocolate and butter and stir until smooth. Stir in the liqueur. Pour the chocolate fondue into a serving bowl or fondue pot and serve warm with accompaniments. If making ahead, refrigerate, covered, for upto one week. Reheat over hot water or in a microwave on medium power, stirring often.

KITCHEN ESSENTIALS

Saucepan
Fondue pot
Fondue forks
Platter for fruits

TIP

To serve – If using an open flame or electric fondue pot, put a few inches of hot water in the pot, and set a bowl containing the chocolate fondue on top. This allows prolonged heating without scorching the chocolate.

Serve leftover chocolate fondue warm over ice cream or with desserts as a chocolate sauce.

HOT CHOCOLATE SOUFFLÉ

Makes 4 small bowls (ramekins)

INGREDIENTS

3 eggs
125 gms butter
125 gms good quality dark chocolate
35 gms flour
150 gms castor sugar
200 ml cream

METHOD

Put the butter and chocolate in a bowl. Melt over a simmering pan of hot water or in the microwave. Whisk the eggs with the sugar.

Add the chocolate and butter. Mix well. Stir in the flour. Divide into 4–5 ramekins or small bowls. Bake at 200ºC for 15-20 minutes until there soufflé's rises. Serve hot. Make a well in the center and pour the cream in.

KITCHEN ESSENTIALS

Oven/Grill
Mixing bowls
Ramekins or small bowls

TIP

The mixture can be made in advance, put into bowls and refrigerated.

SIMPLE CHOCOLATE CAKE

Serves 6

INGREDIENTS

2 cups flour (maida)
2¼ tsps baking powder
2¼ tsps baking soda
1 cup cocoa
2 cups sugar
1 tsp salt
2 eggs
1¼ cups milk
¾ cup oil
1¼ cups boiling water

METHOD

Sift the flour, baking powder, baking soda, cocoa, sugar and salt together and put in a food processor or electric beater.

Add the eggs, milk and oil and mix well (beat). Lastly add the boiling water. Mix and put at once into a 9 inch x 9 inch x 2 inch greased baking tin. Bake for 30 mins at 180ºC.

KITCHEN ESSENTIALS

Oven
Food processor
Baking tin
Serving plate

TIP

This can be made in two tins and sandwiched with chocolate cream / fresh cream.

SWEET NOTHINGS

CHOCOLATE BROWNIES / AMERICAN-STYLE CHEESECAKE / BANANA CAKE

CHOCOLATE BROWNIES

Serves 6-8

INGREDIENTS

1 cup butter
2 cups sugar
4 large eggs
2 tsps vanilla essence
¾ cup cocoa
½ tsp baking powder
¼ tsp salt
1 cup flour
2 cups chopped walnuts

METHOD

Preheat the oven to 180°C.

Grease a baking dish (9 inch x 9 inch x 2 inch.) In a bowl beat the butter and sugar till light. Beat in the eggs one at a time, and add the vanilla.

Add the cocoa powder, baking powder and salt. Fold in the flour and nuts.

Pour into the pan and bake for 30-35 minutes.

KITCHEN ESSENTIALS

Food processor
Baking pan
OTG
Mixing bowl
Serving plate

TIP

The less you fuss about this recipe the better it will turn out. A brownie is actually a failed chocolate cake made by somebody who forgot the baking powder sometime after World War I in the US. The great thing about a perfect brownie is you don't need fancy chocolate; any good cocoa out of a tin is fine. If it is not too dark, add half a teaspoon of instant coffee powder. Do not leave the brownie in the oven for a minute longer than necessary. It should still be gooey in the centre when you take it out. Brownies do not need refrigeration. They stay moist and gooey in an airtight container at room temperature. They should last for a week easily, if you can resist eating them!!!!

AMERICAN-STYLE CHEESECAKE

Serves 6-8

INGREDIENTS

550 gms cream cheese
1cup castor sugar
1 tbsp cornflour
4 eggs
4 tbsps freshly squeezed lime juice
1½ tsp vanilla essence
¼ tsp salt
2 cups cream
8–inch plain sponge cake

METHOD

Preheat the oven to 180°C. Grease an 8 inch x 2 ½ inch or higher spring form tin. Cut the sponge horizontally to about ½ inch thick and line the bottom of the tin with it. Wrap the outside of the tin with a double layer of heavy-duty foil to prevent seepage.

In a large mixing bowl beat the cream cheese and sugar until very smooth (about 3 minutes), preferably with a whisk. Beat in the cornflour. Add the eggs, one at a time, beating after each addition until smooth and scraping down the sides. Add the lime juice, vanilla and salt and beat until incorporated. Beat in the cream just until blended.

Pour the batter into the prepared tin. Set the tin in a larger tin and surround it with one inch of very hot water. Bake for 45 minutes, covered loosely. Turn off the oven without opening the door and let the cake cool in the oven for one hour. Remove and cover with plastic wrap (cling film). Refrigerate.

To unmould: place tin on a heated burner and move it around for 15 seconds or dip into hot water for a few seconds. Wipe sides of tin with a hot, damp towel. Run a thin metal spatula around the sides of the cake and release the sides of the spring form tin.

KITCHEN ESSENTIALS

OTG
Mixing bowl
Baking tin
Serving plate

TIP

For a fruit cheesecake, replace one cup of cream with one cup of fruit purée (mango, banana, strawberry).

BANANA CAKE
Serves 6-8

INGREDIENTS
350 gms bananas, mashed
50 gms walnuts
200 gms flour
1 tsp baking powder
½ tsp soda bicarbonate
½ tsp salt
100 gms butter
200 gms light soft brown sugar
3 eggs, lightly beaten
50 gms cashew nut powder

METHOD
Preheat the oven to 200ºC
Grease a rectangular deep loaf tin and line it with greaseproof paper. Reserve a few nuts for decoration, and then roughly chop the rest. Add the soda bicarbonate, baking powder and salt to the flour. Add the bananas, butter and sugar and mix for two minutes. Gradually add the eggs, then the cashew powder. Turn off and add the chopped walnuts. Pour the mixture into the prepared tin and smoothen the top. Decorate the top with the reserved nuts.
Bake for about 35 mins until well-risen and golden brown. Turn out and cool on a wire rack.

KITCHEN ESSENTIALS
OTG
Food processor
Mixing bowl
Baking tin
Serving plate

TIP
For a better flavour, use really ripe bananas for this recipe, but be sure to process as soon as you peel them.

GLOSSARY

GLOSSARY

Almonds	Badam
Aniseed	Saunf
Asafoetida	Hing
Basil	Italian and Thai. Member of the tulsi family but very different in flavour
Bay leaf	Tejpatta
Bean curd	Tofu
Big green chilli	Bhavnagari mirchi
Bird's eye chilli	lethally spicy chillies
Cardamom	Elaichi
Cheddar cheese	A natural cheese. Melts well on baked dishes
Chickpea flour	Besan
Chironji	Charoli seeds
Cinnamon	Dalchini
Clove	Lavang
Coriander	Dhaniya
Cottage cheese	Paneer
Cream cheese	A soft fresh cream which is slightly salty and sour. Has nothing to do with cheese. If you can't find it readily, can be made by blending paneer and cream with a little salt to a smooth paste in a mixer.
Cumin	Jeera
Currants	Black raisins
Curry leaves	Kadi patta
Curry powder	Use Madras Curry Powder made by Poonjiaji
Dill	Shepu or suva
Flour	Maida
Fried potato straws	Sali
Garlic	Lasan - Wherever mentioned I refer to Chinese garlic (large bulbs) with large cloves
Ginger	Adrak
Guava	Amrudh, peru
Juliennes	Vegetables cut into thin matchstick size strips
Kaffir lime leaves	Leaves of the magrut citrus tree. Used in Thai food. Available dry in some super markets.
Karen Anand's products	**Preserves** – no artificial colour or flavour, made with a minimum of 45 gms fruit per 100 gms **Flavours** – whole strawberry, peach, plum, fig and orange, chunky orange marmalade, mango, banana and orange

	Sauces – spicy Mexican salsa, Italian pasta, noodle stir-fry, Szechwan sauce, noodle stir-fry wholegrain mustard
	Dressings – Italian dressing, French dressing, classic mayonnaise, garlic mayonnaise, eggless mayonnaise, and thousand island
Kidney beans	Rajma
Lemon grass	You can flavour with the whole stalk but when adding chopped to a dish, use the bottom white part only.
Lime	Nimbu
Mace	Javitri
Melon seeds	Magaz
Minced meat	Kheema (mutton, beef or chicken)
Mint	Pudina
Mustard	Rai
Nam Pla	Thai fish sauce - Adds saltiness and flavour to oriental dishes.
Nutmeg	Jaiphal
Olive oil	Many brands available in India today. Use pure olive oil for cooking and extra virgin oil for salads and dips.
Pepper	Kali mirch - Please invest in a pepper mill or grind peppercorns in a mortar and pestle everytime you need to use it. Do not buy commercial powdered white pepper which lacks flavour and is often adulterated.
Processed cheddar cheese	Ideal for cheese sauce
Raisins	Brown kishmish
Red pepper	Red capsicum
Salt	Mota namak is non-iodized sea salt and tastes much better than ordinary table salt. Available at all grocery stores in India and plentiful along the coast from Goa to Kerala. Organic salt, ground sea salt, organic kala namak and organic rock salt are all readily available at supermarkets.
Sesame oil	Til oil
Shallots	Sambar onions
Star anise	Chakri phool

Stock cube	If I was writing this book for accomplished cooks, there would be no doubt that I would ask you to make your own stock. If I ask a young person, fresh into the kitchen to make stock, I guarantee that they would either give up cooking or jump out of the nearest window or both. For them, a stock cube is the only answer.
Sultanas	Yellow raisins
Sun-dried tomatoes	Available dry or in oil
Tahini	A sesame paste readily available in super markets
Tamarind	Imli. Available in fresh, dry and ready pulp form.
Thai ginger	Galangal
Thick cream	Malai
Tom yum paste	A readily available thai paste used for making tom yum soup. Available in super markets
Turmeric	Haldi
Vinegar	Use natural vinegar wherever possible. Imported cider and wine vinegars are available at most super markets. Indian vinegars – malt, apple and toddy vinegars are also available.
Water chestnuts	Singhada (available fresh with a green skin in season, dried with a black skin or in tins)
White poppy seeds	Khuskhus
Yellow pepper	Yellow capsicum
Yellow split lentils	Tuvar dal
Yoghurt	Dahi

STOCKISTS

Shops you can rely on to provide most of the ingredients used in this book. Also given below a list of markets where you can find exotic vegetables and fresh sea food.

In the south, especially in cities like Bangalore and Chennai, a variety of fresh vegetables and sea food is available at most branches of **Nilgiris** and **Food World**

PUNE

DORABJEE'S	Moledina Road
CHANDAN	M.G.Road
GREEN GROCERS	Koregaon Park
OZONE	Aundh
FOOD WORLD	Prabhat Road
SUPER SHOPEE	F C Road
TRUMART	Kondhwa, Shivaji Mk. Senapati Bapat Rd.

Markets

SHIVAJI MARKET	Camp

MUMBAI (by area)

CHEMBUR
CHANDAN DRY FRUIT — ST Road, Chembur Naka

POWAI
HAIKO SUPER MARKET — Hiranandani Complex

GHATKOPAR (EAST)
CHEDAS FOOD KINGDOM — Tilak Road

VILE PARLE (EAST)
9 TO 9 SUPER MARKET — Hanuman Road

SANTACRUZ (WEST)
WILLINGTON SUPER MARKET — Opposite Bombay Mercantile

BANDRA (WEST)
PATEL PROVISION STORE — Near Mehboob Studio

KHAR (WEST)
NEELAM FOOD LAND — Khar Danda Road

JUHU
SPAR SUPERMARKET

WORLI
RAKHANGI'S STORE — Worli Sea Face

CUFFE PARADE
KING PLAZA — Maker Arcade

CRAWFORD MARKET
LUCKY PROVISION STORE — 1/2 Lane

TARDEO	
PYRAMID SUPER MARKET	Cross Roads
COLABA	
SWABAL STORES	Colaba
BREACH CANDY / PEDDAR RD	
ROMAN STORES	Altamount Rd
THE OBEROI DELICATESEN	Nariman Point
WILLINGDON CLUB SHOP	Mahalaxmi
HEALTH SHOP	Peddar Rd
CAFÉ RIDGE	Malabar Hill
FORT	
BOMBAY GYMKHANA CLUB	**FOUNTAIN**
AKBARALLYS HP SPEED MARTS	Bandra (W), Chembur, Nepean Sea Road, Kala Ghoda
D`MART	Powai, Thane, Kandivali (E) & (W), Nerul & Vashi, Malad
BIG BAZAR	High St Phoenix (Lower Parel), Vashi, Mulund, Andheri (W), Malad(W), Goregaon

Markets

CRAWFORD MARKET	
COLABA MARKET	
PALI HILL MARKET	
CITYLIGHT (SEAFOOD),	Mahim
GRANT ROAD (SEAFOOD)	
BIG CATCH (SEAFOOD)	Pali Hill

HYDERABAD

Q-MART	Jubilee Hills
RATNADEEP SUPER MARKET	Vikrampuri & Srinagar Colony
TARAKARI	Banjar Hills, Road No.1
CONTEMPORARY ARTS & CRAFTS	Punjagutta `X` Roads
SECUNDERABAD CLUB	Secunderabad
BALAJI GRAND BAZAR	Basheerbagh & Masab Tank

Tarakari & Pure O Natural stock exotic vegetables and seafood.

BANGALORE

NILGIRIS	Brigade Road
SUNDAY TO MONDAY	Indiranagar
FOOD WORLD	At all outlets
NAMDARI	Jay Nagar
SEVEN ELEVEN	Jay Nagar
METRO	Yeshwantpura
ALL SAINTS	Brigade Road
FAB MALL	J P Nagar

Market
RUSSELL MARKET

CHENNAI

AMMA NANA	R.A. Puram
NUTS `N` SPICES	Adyar
IN & OUT	Anna Nagar
AIWO	Nungambakkam
MARMALADE	Khader Nawaz Khan Road
CAKES & BAKES	At all outlets
NILGIRIS	All outlets
FOOD WORLD	All outlets
AHUMCAARA	Kilpauk

Markets

PANAGAL PARK	T Nagar
PAZHAMUDIR CHOLAI	All outlets
SURIYA SWEETS	RA Puram

KOLKATTA

SRI SRI DEPT	Salt Lake
SRI SRI STORES	Elgin Road
SATURDAY CLUB	Theatre road
HEALTH FOOD CENTRE	Theatre road
POOJA FISCAL	Tolly Road

Markets
NEWMARKET

GOA

KITCHEN NET SUPER MARKET	Madgaon
BORKAR STORES	Madgaon
MAGSON STORES	Panjim
CALANGUTE SUPER MARKET	Calangute
PARKET SUPER STORES	Mapusa
FARMER'S BASKETS	Mapusa

Markets

MAPUSA MARKET	
TINTO	Calangute
PANAJI MARKET	
MARGAO MARKET	

DELHI

ANAND STORES	Khan Market
SALUJA STORES	
GYMKHANA STORES	

SARDARJI	
DEFENCE STORES	Defence Colony Market
GURGAON	